BULLETS AND BEIGNETS

A SEASIDE FRENCH PATISSERIE MYSTERY
BOOK 3

KAT BELLEMORE

KB PRESS

CHOOSE YOUR OWN ADVENTURE: MYSTERY OR ROMANCE

MADDIE SWALLOWS MYSTERIES:

New Mexican Cozy Mystery

Dead Before Dinner

Dead Upon Arrival

Dead Before I Do

Dead Among Stars

Dead by Design

Dead in the Dark

Dead Without a Hitch

Dead by the Outlaw's Noose

SEASIDE FRENCH PATISSERIE MYSTERIES

Death and Dacquoise

Poison and Pudding

Bullets and Beignets

Murder and Madeleines

BORROWING AMOR: New Mexican Romance

Borrowing Amor

Borrowing Love

1

I blamed Hollywood for my current predicament. They created movies that seemed so magical and effortless, when the reality was far from it. No one had warned me about the endless hours of sitting. And standing. And waiting. So. Much. Waiting.

I squirmed in my seat, hoping the director would be ready for us soon. What kind of person made an old woman sit in a metal folding chair for this long? My muscles had stopped working an hour earlier, and there was no way I would be able to get out of the chair without help.

I turned to the young man who sat next to me. He was on the thin side, but his arms seemed toned enough.

When he noticed me staring, I asked, "Are you stronger than you look?"

He glanced around at the other background actors—

there were around thirty of us—as if wondering if anyone else had noticed the crazy old lady who was asking personal questions. They weren't paying attention, but that was probably because they were all used to me by now. Erwin was sitting at the end of my row, feeding his dog, Donna. Apparently, they had been hired as a package deal, but Erwin wasn't getting paid any more than the rest of us. It was too bad; otherwise, I would have tried to get Dottie's cat, Skittles, hired. Of course, that cat would have been terrible at following directions.

Our doctor, Patty, sat in the row behind me. The production team had wanted to hire her to be on set as medical support, but when she'd discovered she couldn't both do medical support and participate as an extra in the movie, she'd told them they could find someone else to put Band-Aids on people. If she was going to hang around the set, she wanted to at least have some fun doing it. I didn't blame her one bit for that.

My attention returned to the young man. He was nervously running a hand through his dark hair. It was longer than I thought looked good, like he was two weeks past due for a haircut.

"I need to know if you exercise at least three times a week," I said to him. "It won't do either of us any good if you get injured while helping me."

"Helping you?" he echoed, his brows furrowed in confusion.

"Yes. I need your help," I said, trying to hide my impatience. "I was told to be at the community center two hours ago. We haven't done a darn thing in all that time, and somewhere along the way, I've gotten stuck."

The young man's confusion gave way to panic. "I think they have a medic somewhere around here—"

I held up a hand, stopping him before he could go any further. "Yes, there is one on set, but that doesn't do me any good because he's all the way down the hill at the beach where they are shooting today's scenes."

"Isn't she a doctor?" the young man asked, gesturing behind us toward Dr. Patty, who was reading a book. "She could help you." He looked hopeful.

I gave him a patient smile. "Patty is wonderful at what she does—really, she's the best doctor I've ever had—but she's in no shape to be able to lift this..." I gestured to myself. Over the past couple of years, since opening Sand-castle Bakery with Dottie, I'd gained a few pounds, mostly in the midsection. I considered it an occupational hazard —someone had to sample the pastries for quality control.

"It's true," Patty chimed in. She put down her book and leaned forward. "I really have no upper body strength. All brains and no brawn. I hire a medical assistant for that kind of thing."

The young man's gaze darted between Patty and me. "That may be, but I don't think I could—"

"Now, before you start judging me for letting myself go," I interrupted. "I know it might not look like it, but I exercise regularly. Once a week I do yoga, one day is parkour, and the third day, I go on a long walk with my sister Dottie and her cat, Skittles. We put a leash on her so she doesn't get into trouble. On Skittles, not Dottie."

"I wasn't—"

"Even so, as you get older," I continued, "you'll find that your muscles don't work like they used to." I patted my blue hair—I'd dyed it the evening before. The production designer hadn't been thrilled when she'd seen it, but there hadn't been much she could do about it at that point. "I know I probably look closer to fifty, but you give me a metal chair with no support and forget about me for two hours, and my body starts to rebel." I eyed his forearm. "May I?"

He gave a tentative nod, I'm sure having no idea what he was agreeing to.

I poked his forearm, and sure enough, pure muscle. "You'll have no problem of it. As soon as the director says he's ready for us, you be ready to pull."

The young man swallowed hard, once again looking around. No one else was going to volunteer, nor would I ask them to. I knew every one of them—and I didn't trust them not to drop me. By accident or otherwise.

"Okay," the young man finally said. I patted his hand in a grandmotherly way and smiled. "Thank you, dear. That's so kind of you." As if he'd had a choice.

He gave a weak nod.

"I'm Jo, by the way. Jo Darby." And I stuck out a hand.

The young man took my hand and shook it. "Blake Sommer."

"You aren't from around here, are you, Blake? I've never seen you before."

He shook his head slowly. "No. When I heard that Eli Hunt was filming a movie less than three hours from where I live, I knew I had to try to get on set. The three-hour drive is worth being here."

"Yes, he's quite famous, isn't he? At least that's what my pastry chef, Autumn, tells me. She and I watched some of Eli Hunt's previous movies so I could be prepared for my first day on set, but I have to say, this wasn't at all what I was expecting. You always hear about the magic of Hollywood, and there's all that behind-the-scenes footage, but the most magic I've seen today was when that costume lady said she liked the blue outfit I'd brought with me rather than the red one I was wearing. Apparently, the camera doesn't like red. Good thing they asked us to bring some alternative outfits." I paused. "I suppose it wasn't exactly magical, but I did agree with her. The blue really brings out my eyes, don't you think?" I turned so Blake could see.

"They sure do," he said, then he shifted in his seat, as if he were counting down the minutes to when we'd be called to film our scene. I understood the feeling—it was rather dull sitting here for so long. Good thing Blake had sat next to me and I could help him pass the time with conversation. Most everyone else was on their phones, not even bothering to talk to their neighbors.

"Do you know the screenwriter, Leanne Warner?" I asked. "She lives right here in Starlight Ridge. That's how Eli Hunt ended up filming his movie here. It's very exciting for all of us. Even Isaac. We weren't sure that Isaac and Leanne would get back together after she was gone for so long. They were engaged to be married, you know, and then she ran off to Hollywood for two years. It took some doing, but after Isaac had a terrible surfing accident, they patched things up. Nothing brings together two people like a near-death experience, am I right?"

Blake nodded. "You're right."

"Of course he's in a wheelchair right now. It should probably only be another month or so, though. He's itching to get back on a surfboard. And to get married. He wants to be out of that wheelchair for both."

A pause.

I realized I was going to have to be the one to carry the conversation. Blake appeared to be the strong, silent type.

"Did you drive your own car here?" I asked.

"I did," he said. "Your town isn't exactly accessible by public transportation. Besides, I'd never leave my car unattended for longer than a couple days. If even one person caught wind that I was out of town, I hate to think what might happen to it."

"What kind of car is it?"

Blake's eyes lit up, and it was obvious how much he

loved his car. Finally, something we could talk about. "A 2014 VW Beetle GSR."

"Wow, that's a nice one," I said, though I knew nothing about cars. If Blake was excited about it, though, I would be too.

"It's more than nice. It's rare. Only thirty-five hundred of them were made worldwide. It's yellow with black stripes, a tribute to the original 1970 GSR Beetle. Except this one has a turbocharged engine."

The door in front of us opened, saving me from having to pretend I understood a thing Blake was talking about. A young woman appeared in the doorway, a clipboard in her hands. She called for us to follow her out to the shuttle that would take us to the filming location. I thought it silly that we had to use a shuttle—we were filming on the beach, and it was only a ten-minute walk—but there was a certain way things were done when making a movie, and apparently that included shuttles.

"Did they tell you?" I asked Blake as he leaped from his seat, obviously relieved that we were finally done waiting. "When we get down there, the beach is going to be set up like we're attending a large town festival. I honestly couldn't be happier, because I won't need to act for it—it's like a regular Tuesday evening. The only difference, of course, is that a famous movie star will be there."

"I did hear that, yes." And then Blake offered me his arm.

I grabbed hold of it, and he pulled me up to my feet. He

had been a good choice—he acted as if I didn't weigh a thing. Even so, my breaths came fast at the exertion of getting up, and I patted his arm. "When we're done filming for the day, please come by Sandcastle Bakery. I want to give you one of our pastries as a thank you."

Blake smiled for the first time since I'd met him. It was a half-smile, like it was something he wasn't used to doing. "I'll have to take you up on that."

I squeezed his arm, then pushed ahead through the crowd. The clipboard woman stopped in front of the shuttle doors, and we all stopped with her. Even from there, I could see the cameras and lights that were set up on the beach, waiting for us to arrive. I was surprised by just how many people were down there, milling around and checking the equipment. Maybe this was what people meant when they referred to the magic of Hollywood— how a process that was as complex as this could come across to the viewer as effortless.

"It's good you came for us when you did," I told the woman as she waited for a few stragglers. "We were sitting in there an awful long time."

She gave a forced smile—I could tell she was exhausted. She had probably arrived at the community center far earlier than we had. "I know it's a tedious process, but it would have taken much longer if we hadn't had all of you ready and on standby." The women then raised her clipboard in the air and called to the group. "As you board the shuttle, I'm going to have each of you tell me your name. This is important because if you are not checked off on my list, it means you weren't here, and you won't get paid." She gestured toward the shuttle. "You can take a seat anywhere."

More sitting? I wasn't falling for that again. I shook my head and told her, "Thanks. I think I'll stand."

The woman shrugged, like she didn't care either way. "It's up to you, but it's not the smoothest of rides."

The doors opened, and after giving the woman my name, I walked past all the seats to the end of the shuttle. Everyone quickly sat down, and I held on to the back of Erwin's seat, spreading my feet in a wide stance, determined to not be thrown off balance when the bus started. Erwin's dog, Donna, sat next to him, perched on her hind legs as she looked out the window.

The young woman, who was evidently in charge, was the last to board, and she remained standing at the front by the driver. She held up an arm, asking for our attention, and the murmurs that had broken out quieted.

"Welcome to day twelve of the filming of *Amaretto*. I am Jennifer Cole, and I'm the production assistant." She paused, as if that was supposed to mean something. When no one said anything, she continued. "You've all received at least one or two emails from me, so you have my contact information. If an emergency arises and you can't come on one of your scheduled days, or if you're in need of anything while on set, please let me know immediately, and I'll do my best to take care of you."

Erwin raised his hand. "I've gotten locked out of my email because I forgot the password. Can you print off my schedule for me?"

"Just change your password," Patty shouted from where she was seated in the front. "There's literally a link that says 'forgot my password.'"

"Even that asks for a lot of information," Erwin called back. He turned to Jennifer. "Could you help me reset my password?"

Patty caught my eye and gave me a dramatic side eye, like she couldn't believe this guy. "I'm sure that's not what Jennifer meant when she said she could help with anything."

"Yes it is," Erwin insisted, "because I can't get my schedule."

Jennifer looked like she was rethinking her life choices as she tried to regain control of the shuttle. "You will be filming one scene today," she half-shouted, trying to be heard. "Most of you will be in a total of two to three scenes over the next six weeks. Please refer to the schedule I emailed you for your future call times. Remember, all dates and times are tentative. Please plan on being flexible." She looked at Erwin. "And if you can't access your email, please find a friend who can help you with that."

I assumed Jennifer did not want to be that friend.

According to my schedule, I would be in three scenes. One took place at a town festival—this scene—one at

Adeline's chocolate shop, and the third... Well, I had questions about that one.

I raised my hand.

Jennifer didn't seem to want to call on me, probably thinking I'd ask her to change my password too, but eventually, she nodded to me. "Yes?"

"I'm Jo Darby. We spoke earlier?"

"Yes, I remember you, Jo."

"I have a question about the third scene I'm supposed to be in. I believe it's in about a month."

Jenifer didn't say anything, waiting for me to continue.

"Well, it's just—do you think people will really believe that a woman like me spends her free time at a bar? I'm assuming the scene takes place in the evening after eight o'clock, which just so happens to be when I'm getting ready for bed."

Jennifer seemed unsure how to respond to that. "You're worried that people will wonder what you're doing up so late?" she finally asked.

I laughed, realizing how that must have come across. "Oh, no, although now that you mention it, it is something to consider." I paused, wondering how best to phrase this. "I know I don't have all of the information about what the scene entails, but I imagine that if I walked into a bar after eight o'clock, half the people there would be thinking, 'What's my grandma doing here?' I mean, nobody wants to have a beer with their grandmother, do they?"

Jennifer studied me, looking amused. "You think you're

too old to be in a bar scene. Last time I checked, older women do drink alcohol."

"We do," I conceded, "but I'm at the stage of life where I relax with a glass of wine at home. My friends and I like to socialize, but we don't feel the need to go somewhere dark and loud to do it."

Jennifer eyed my blue hair. "Good thing you aren't in the bar scene as yourself, then. It's called acting."

I saw what was going on here—they'd placed me in the scene because they thought I would do well as the 'hip grandma' type.

"The hair fooled you, didn't it," I said.

Jennifer gave me a placating smile. "It wasn't my call. I'm just the production assistant, making sure things run smoothly." She glanced at her phone. "That includes keeping on schedule, so—"

Jennifer was cut off when a thunderous boom shuddered through the bus.

2

The bus shook, and I threw myself onto the floor, covering my head. I hadn't moved that fast in a decade.

Once it seemed the danger was over, I slowly pushed myself up. Jennifer had already run out the shuttle door while everyone else crowded around the windows. I used Erwin's seat to pull myself up off the floor and then joined him and Donna at the window, half-expecting to see rubble, flames, and ash.

Instead, everything looked normal.

Embarrassment flooded through me when I realized I'd just thrown myself onto the floor and there had been no real danger. This was just another one of those Hollywood moments. Controlled explosions were what the movie business was known for, after all, though I hadn't realized this was that type of movie. I was fairly certain this was supposed to be a romance.

Jennifer, however, must have seen something I hadn't, because outside the shuttle, she looked panicked. She paced outside, speaking rapidly into her radio, her gaze always returning to the same spot at the bottom of the hill. I moved to join her outside, but Patty intervened—as much as she'd wanted to escape it, she was now in full doctor mode.

"You okay, Jo?" she asked, looking me over for any obvious sign of injury. "You hit the floor pretty hard."

"I think so, though I'm sure I'll be sore tomorrow."

Patty gave a satisfied nod, like she could have told me as much. "I don't want you on set. Go home and rest. I'm sure Dottie and Autumn can handle the bakery for the rest of the day."

They could. But then they'd make a bigger fuss over me than the situation warranted. I didn't need someone checking on me every thirty minutes. And I certainly didn't need to miss out on my first day as a background actor. I was fine.

"I'll make sure to get the rest I need," I assured her, knowing that any other answer would just lead to an argument, which I'd lose. What I didn't tell her was that I'd get the rest after we were finished here for the day.

I gave her a little wave, not at all intending to go home, and stepped outside, curious what had Jennifer all panicked.

I turned toward the beach, and my breath caught in my throat.

At the bottom of the hill, smoke billowed from a trailer that sat on the beach. Thankfully no buildings were damaged, but debris was scattered in a large radius around the burned-out trailer. It would take a community initiative to get all that cleaned up. After the sheriff and our volunteer fire chief were done with it, of course.

Jennifer appeared beside me. "That was Christopher's trailer." When I raised a questioning eyebrow, she clarified, "Our director."

"He chose to stay in that, rather than the bed and breakfast?" I asked. Any motor home I'd ever stayed in left my back aching for the next two months.

Jennifer nodded. "Expensive trailers like that are more comfortable than you realize and they are customized to the individual. Not only that, but Christopher values his privacy—it's important in his line of work."

I supposed that made sense. "I'm surprised he's the only one who brought his trailer, if privacy is what he was after."

"Eli Hunt brought his," Jennifer said, nodding to the far side of the beach. "You can't see it, but it's parked way out there, on the other end of town." She glanced at me. "He's a method actor, you know, and expects us all to respect the process. He said it would be more difficult if he was surrounded by friends when he wasn't on set."

"It's a good thing he wanted that space," I said. "If his

trailer had been parked next to Christopher's, it could have been a chain reaction." I paused, and bit my lip, nervous to ask the question that must have been on her mind. "Do you think—"

"No, Christopher wasn't in his trailer," Jennifer said with a vigorous shake of her head. "At least...I don't think so. Just ten minutes ago, he radioed and said that Eli was finishing up a scene on the boardwalk and he wanted all of you to be in place when they arrived at the new location."

I should have been relieved, but lingering thoughts pestered me. What if Christopher had had to quickly grab something from his trailer before walking over? What if he'd asked Eli Hunt to do it for him and the famous actor had been caught in the explosion instead?

"Has anyone been in contact with Eli or Christopher since the explosion?" I asked, my words slow.

Jennifer hesitated, her lips pulling into a frown. "I don't know. Right after the explosion, my radio went crazy, everyone talking at once, trying to figure out what had happened. The one question everyone kept asking was if anyone had eyes on Christopher, and from what I could tell, the answer was, no. Of course, it was so chaotic, I quickly realized that no one knew anything at all, and their fear was perpetuating more fear. I ultimately gave up and turned the radio off."

"Did anyone ask about Eli?" I asked.

"No," Jennifer said with a shake of her head. "But

Christopher and Eli are always together. Where you find one, you'll find the other."

Erwin stuck his head out from the shuttle. "Do you know if we're heading down to set soon? I don't want to be *that* person, it's just that Donna needs to relieve herself, and I don't know if I should take her out now or wait until we get down there."

Jennifer glanced his way, her gaze blank, as if she wasn't processing what he was saying.

I touched her lightly on the sleeve. "Are we still filming today?"

She looked to her radio, as if it would have the answers. "I don't know." And then she hurried back into the community center, muttering to herself as she went.

I was pretty sure the answer was going to be no, but it wasn't Jennifer's call to make.

"Good news, Donna," Erwin said, "You can use the bathroom now," and they exited the shuttle, moving off into some rocks for the dog to do her business.

I turned to follow Jennifer inside, but paused when I heard a car racing up the hill toward the community center. My breath caught. It had to be the director driving up here with Eli Hunt. They were okay. I spun toward the car as it screeched to a stop in front of me, the windows down.

It wasn't them.

Dottie's eyes were wide with terror. Her gaze landed on me, and her whole body melted in relief. "You're okay." Her lips trembled as she tried to maintain her composure. "We all felt the explosion, and then people were talking about it happening near the movie set and I—"

"I'm fine," I told her, trying not to show how scared I had been and how shaken I still was. "We hadn't left yet." I nodded toward the smoke that still spiraled into the sky. "The same can't be said for the director's trailer." I didn't tell her that Christopher and Eli were still unaccounted for.

"Let's go," Dottie said, motioning for me to get in the car. "Deputy Randy is already putting up barricades down at the beach. The fire chief is on site, and I have no doubt that Sheriff Hart is on his way. We'll want to get home before the entire boardwalk is closed off."

I glanced back at the community center, my guilty conscience telling me I shouldn't leave—I should help. But what could I do here? Patty had already told me to go home for the day, and Dottie was right, there was no way they would be able to continue filming. Sheriff Hart wouldn't allow it. I opened the car door and slid into the passenger seat.

Even after I'd closed the door, Dottie sat quietly, making no move to drive us home. Tears sprang to her eyes. "I thought..."

I pulled her into an awkward side hug. "I know. But I'm okay. Really."

Our eldest sister had died a couple of years earlier—she'd been murdered, actually—and I could only imagine what Dottie had been feeling, her thoughts spiraling as she confronted the possibility that she would have to deal with the sudden death of her other sister, and this time on her own.

But I was okay.

I kept repeating the words to myself, hoping to convince myself that it really had not been that big a deal. Like I hadn't been minutes away from being on set near the explosion.

I'm okay.

I'm okay.

I'm okay.

"What do you think caused it?" Dottie asked, interrupting my thoughts. The panic had faded, and her hard expression told me she had turned off the emotions and moved into police mode. "Faulty wiring? I have several friends who have returned their RVs because of safety issues."

She was trying to distract herself from what could have been—focusing on something logical. Concrete.

"Maybe," I said, also needing the distraction.

I saw Jennifer re-emerge from the community center and approach the shuttle. It wasn't another minute before everyone was filing off. Looked like she had been able to get ahold of someone and she was sending everyone home.

"It could also have been the refrigerator," I added.

Dottie glanced at me, an eyebrow raised. "Refrigerator?"

I nodded, my attention returning to her. "There's a type of refrigerator that runs on propane, weirdly enough, and RVs use them. There's been a lot of problems and tons of recalls, though. I don't know if trailers as fancy as these would bother with them—they're way too dangerous."

Dottie's lips twitched up into a smile. "You've been reading *RV Today* again, haven't you?"

I folded my arms across my chest, immediately defensive. "Maybe I have. It's not like I subscribed to it—they automatically started sending it to me when I turned sixty. What was I going to do, throw it away and waste a perfectly good magazine?"

"And then they kept sending it to you, even after you moved here to California?"

I bit back a guilty smile. "I may have provided them with our new address, but RVs really are the best way to see the country."

"You don't even drive," Dottie pointed out.

"No, but you do."

She didn't have a rebuttal to that, and instead shifted the car into drive and did a U-turn.

It was quiet as we drove back down the hill toward the boardwalk.

"I don't want you participating in this movie," she finally said, breaking the silence.

That didn't surprise me. Dottie had always been fiercely protective of me.

"One guy's propane tank explodes, and I'm supposed to walk away from my debut on the big screen?" I protested. "I'm never going to have another chance like this. Eli Hunt is one of the world's biggest stars, and I get to be in three scenes with him." I saw that Dottie was about to interrupt, so I spoke faster, not giving her the chance. "And it's not just about me. I'm supporting Leanne—it's her big debut as a screenwriter, and I want to be a part of that."

Dottie released a long sigh. "I know, but if these Hollywood guys take such poor care of their own trailers—"

And radios, I thought.

"—do you think it's going to be any better on the actual movie set? Those Hollywood people are only looking out for themselves. Even if a set is dangerous, they'll push on, if it means getting the shot they need and staying on schedule."

"You're overreacting," I said. "It's not like I'm in a car chase or leaping from exploding buildings. There are going to be zero pyrotechnics. I'm literally standing in the background buying a box of chocolates, or walking along the beach."

Or sitting in a bar. I hadn't told Dottie about that one. I didn't think she'd approve.

"You mean the same beach where a trailer just exploded?" Dottie asked.

I could hear the *I just proved my point* in her voice, but I chose to ignore it, mostly because Dottie had turned the corner and couldn't drive any farther.

The road was blocked by barricades and people.

Up the road was the town's only fire engine, spraying the still-smoking trailer, and Sheriff Hart, pacing in front of it. He was on his phone, his arms waving wildly as he had an animated conversation with someone.

"I'd hoped we'd beat the chaos," Dottie said, parking the car. "Guess we're walking from here." She stepped out of the car, and I followed suit. As we got closer to the commotion, the air was tense, as should be expected after an explosion.

Our town's chocolate shop owner, Adeline, stood at one of the barriers, chewing her nails and looking anxious. Her shop was on the boardwalk and directly across from the beach, and I wondered if she'd witnessed the whole thing. If the shrapnel had traveled farther, she could have been injured, or worse. No wonder she was shaken up.

I left Dottie and walked over. "You okay, Addie?"

Adeline tried to smile, but it failed, and she instead shook her head. "I knew something like this was going to happen. Wherever Hollywood goes, chaos follows."

I had heard rumors that Adeline's father was an actor, but he had left Addie's family when she was little and they hadn't had contact with him since. Her mom had moved on to the next famous actor and had left Adeline alone. I was sure having Hollywood come to Starlight Ridge was dredging up all sorts of difficult feelings for her.

"At least no one got hurt," I said, hoping it was true.

Addie whipped to me in surprise. "But Jo, someone did get hurt." She nodded to an area about twenty feet from the trailer.

A still figure lay in the sand.

My heart stalled. I had no idea if it was Christopher or Eli Hunt, but he was being loaded onto a stretcher, the majority of his body burned from the explosion.

Even from this distance, I could tell that the man wasn't just injured, though.

He was dead.

3

I felt a hand on my arm and glanced over at Dottie. She had moisture in her eyes, a rarity for her, and she tugged me away.

"We need to move along. I'm sure Autumn needs us back at the bakery." She tried to keep her voice steady—it didn't work.

I knew it wasn't the director's death specifically that was so upsetting for her, it was this scene. The burned-out trailer. The body. When she had been on the police force, there had been many scenes like this one. And ones that were far worse. She didn't talk about it often, but when she did, she got like this. Quiet. Sad. Like the images still haunted her.

"Okay, Dottie. Let's go." I turned to follow her but stopped when I heard a man's voice ringing above the murmurs of the crowd.

"My God, it's so much worse than I thought."

A tall man wearing plaid pants and an overcoat pushed through the crowd and hopped over one of the barricades. Sheriff Hart rushed forward to stop him from getting any closer, but the man merely shrugged him off.

"That is my trailer, and I have the right to know what happened." His gaze landed on the body that lay on a stretcher nearby, and he fell to his knees.

My gaze whipped to Dottie, and she knew exactly what I was thinking.

"No, Jo. Don't go within a hundred miles of this thing."

"But the man in the overcoat—that must be Christopher, the director of the movie. So, who is that?" I pointed to the deceased.

Eli Hunt. It had to be.

Dottie shook her head and continued to pull on me. "That's for the sheriff to figure out. Because, unlike you, he takes his job seriously."

I frowned. "I take my job at the bakery very seriously."

Dottie's lips twitched up at the edges. "Yes, until something more interesting comes along."

I wanted to protest and tell Dottie she was being unfair, but unfortunately, I knew she was right.

"What if someone from town was killed?" I tried one more time. "Don't you think we should stick around to find out?"

That thought gave Dottie pause, but then she shook her head for a second time. "You saw how badly burned the body is. Identification is going to take time. We should go."

And then she turned and walked away.

Grudgingly, I followed.

Not without a final glance toward the crime scene, though. I saw the sheriff bend down and pick something up. He showed it to Christopher, who shook his head.

What I would give to know what that object was.

"I DON'T KNOW why we're bothering to stay open today," I said, sulking at the counter. "Everyone is preoccupied with the explosion, and no one is going to be in the mood for pastries."

Our bakery was decorated for the holidays, garlands and lights draping the counters. It was easy to forget that Christmas was just around the corner. And not just because we lived in a coastal town that rarely saw snow.

The movie that was being filmed, *Amaretto*, was supposed to take place during the spring, which meant that Starlight Ridge was unable to have the customary decorations hanging from the streetlamps or in the shops along the boardwalk.

Dottie and I had tried to do what we could here, but with all the chaos that came with filming a movie, and the fact that it was sixty-five degrees outside, it was difficult to get into the Christmas spirit.

And now, with the explosion and someone dying?

It was going to be next to impossible.

Autumn was sitting next to me at the counter, her hands propping up her chin. She looked like she was about to fall asleep. "I agree with Jo. We haven't had a single customer all morning. Let's just close up and try again tomorrow. Maybe by then the intrigue will have worn off and it will be business as usual."

Dottie spun toward us and snapped, "Someone has died. It shouldn't be business as usual." Her expression was pulled tight in anger.

Autumn sat up and opened her mouth, but no words came out. Dottie never spoke to anyone that way, especially Autumn.

Dottie immediately regretted it, and her expression softened. "I'm sorry Autumn. Today—it's been a lot for me. But that's no excuse to be rude."

"It's okay, I understand," Autumn said quietly, though I could tell she didn't.

"It's from her time as a cop," I whispered to Autumn when Dottie had turned her back on us. I could tell that Dottie was trying to hide how upset she was with herself. Whenever she got in these moods, she was much harder on herself than anyone else ever could be. "She saw some really awful things that she won't tell even me about. It's best just to give her love on days like today. And to not take anything she says personally."

Autumn nodded, but she still eyed Dottie warily, like

she was afraid she'd accidentally do something that would get her yelled at again.

"Let's go for a walk," I said to Dottie, trying to sound cheerful. "We'll take Skittles to the bed and breakfast. Leanne always has those mints you like on the front counter. And maybe we can grab some lunch while we're there. It's Thursday, which means its enchiladas."

Dottie still had her back to us as she wiped at her eyes, and then she turned, her back straight and her head held high. "Yes, let's do that. Leanne is the only person in town who gives Skittles a can of tuna when we eat there. Everyone else just gives her the stink eye."

"To be fair, they have a right to be worried about cat hair getting in their food," Autumn said, before her eyes widened and she immediately clamped her lips shut, like she hadn't meant to speak.

I hated to see her like this—afraid of Dottie. But Autumn was going to see this side of my sister sooner or later, and it was better that it happened while I was here. It wasn't Dottie's fault, and it wasn't Autumn's. It was simply something that was.

"Very true," I said. "Skittles isn't known for behaving around food, which I suppose is ironic considering..." I gestured in a wide circle to the pastries that surrounded us in display cases.

"Which is another reason to take this walk," Autumn said. "She behaves much better at the bakery when we've taken her out and she's able to burn off all that excess energy."

Dottie snorted. "That's cute that you think Skittles ever runs out of energy. She just lies low, waiting for us to get comfortable. She's a devious one, she is."

Autumn gave her a hesitant smile. "That she is."

As if on cue, Skittles appeared at the bottom of the staircase that led to our apartment. She looked between the three of us, then let out a long yawn and stretch before giving us a little meow, like she'd heard us talking.

I smiled. "I think Skittles is very much in favor of a walk."

"You get the harness and leash on Skittles, and I'll meet you outside," Dottie said. "I'd help, but my knees have been acting up."

She said the same thing every day—*I'd help, but my knees have been acting up*. It had become such a habit, I wondered if she ever considered the truthfulness of the statement before she said it. I knew her knees weren't what they had been when she was forty, but I also knew she could do more than she thought she could.

"No problem. I can help," Autumn said, sliding off her stool, almost as if it were a peace offering. Like she was trying to make up for something.

Dottie thanked her, then left the bakery to sit outside and wait for us. I turned to Autumn. "You didn't do anything wrong, you know."

"But she's right," Autumn insisted, picking up Skittles

and then sitting down in a chair. She held the cat as I slipped the harness on. Skittles was used to the process and didn't fight, much. She had learned that sitting still for the harness meant she got to go on a walk. "I was callous. Someone has died—and we don't even know who. Whether it was someone on the film crew or one of us in town, their death isn't something we hope people get over so they'll buy beignets."

"I suppose," I said. "It is difficult, though, when we don't have any information. We can't exactly mourn a rich man's trailer, can we?" I clipped Skittles' leash onto the harness. "Someone at the bed and breakfast might know more—that's where most of the film crew is staying. Then we can properly pay our respects."

Autumn seemed lightened by the plan and set Skittles down, firmly holding the leash. "We better get walking, then. We have a man to mourn."

"And enchiladas to eat," I added as I locked up the bakery. When Autumn raised an eyebrow, I said, "It doesn't do anyone any good being sad on an empty stomach."

Autumn couldn't argue with that logic.

BY THE TIME we reached the bed and breakfast, I could tell Dottie was already feeling better. We'd had to walk up a fairly steep hill, and the physical exertion had done all of us a bit of good.

I turned and surveyed the ocean in front of us.

"Beautiful," Dottie murmured, walking up next to me. "Just beautiful. I'll never get used to this view."

"And we shouldn't," I said. "I want to be surprised by it every day."

As if the universe had heard but misunderstood me, the door to the bed and breakfast flung open behind us, causing all three of us to jump.

I turned to see a slender man standing in the doorway. He had graying slicked-back hair, his lips pulled into a frown.

"I expected better, Leanne," he said, stepping out onto the porch. "It's because of me that you have this opportunity. I am your mentor, and now you're banning me from set? It's bad enough that I've been relegated to a tiny room in the farthest corner of this godforsaken hotel, as if you're hiding me away. The cameramen and lighting crew have better views than I do. But this..."

Leanne stepped into view, visibly frustrated. "It's not a punishment. I truly appreciate all you've done for me, Frederick, but this isn't your movie. I wrote the screenplay, and I will be making any revisions that need to be made." Frederick opened his mouth to speak, but Leanne held up a finger, cutting him off. "Before you say anything, those revisions—they aren't your call. They are Christopher's. You literally have no say in it, and some people—they feel like you're overstepping. I agree with them. Handing me the script with your red scribbles on every page was completely inappropriate."

"Then what am I even doing here?" he snapped.

"That is a question I've asked myself several times." She paused, holding up one hand when she saw Frederick's expression tighten. "I'll always appreciate you helping me make the connections I did. You gave me wonderful advice when I was cleaning up *Amaretto's* script. But you acted as an advisor. Not a co-writer. The life that this screenplay has taken on—it's no longer yours."

Frederick's eyes narrowed. "You're not just banning me from set. You want me to leave town."

Leanne hesitated, but then her posture straightened. "I'm sorry, Frederick, but you're getting in the way and slowing production."

"If that's true, why hasn't anyone said something before now?" He took a step toward Leanne, as if challenging her.

"Because they know how influential you are, and they're all too scared of you," Leanne said, standing her ground. "No one wants to be blacklisted by Frederick Alberheist."

"Apparently, you don't care if you are," Frederick said. "You deem yourself the hero by taking me on."

Leanne didn't even flinch. "I stopped being scared of you a long time ago, Freddy. That doesn't make me a hero."

Frederick bristled at the obviously unwanted nickname. "You're right. It makes you stupid. Because you should be scared."

And then he leaped down the stairs of the wraparound porch and strode past the three of us with a strength that belied his age. With a slam of his car door, he roared off in a sleek black Lamborghini.

"Oh, dear," I said. "I'm afraid we might have come at a bad time."

Autumn agreed. "Remind me to never pick a fight with that guy."

I thought back to Christopher's burned-out trailer.

Maybe someone already had.

4

L eanne watched the black car until it was out of sight, and then her gaze landed on the three of us, her lips opening in surprise. She returned her gaze to the horizon, as if making sure the man was actually gone, before her whole body slumped in exhaustion. "I'm sorry you had to see that. Frederick... He's a lot."

"I'll say," Autumn said. "Who was that guy?"

Leanne gestured for us to follow her inside. "Frederick Alberheist. He was my mentor when I was living in LA."

"He sure thinks a lot of himself," Dottie said, frowning. She held onto the banister as she slowly made her way up the porch steps. "And not much of anyone else, it seems."

I pointed out the accessibility ramp to the left of us, but Dottie waved me off.

"For good reason," Leanne said. "The movie industry hails Frederick as one of the greatest screenwriters of all time. He knows he's untouchable." She held out a hand to help Dottie up the last step. Dottie surprised me by taking it. "And I hate to admit it, but Frederick was right about one thing. My screenplay wouldn't have been picked up by Eli Hunt if it weren't for Frederick's influence and connections."

"That's still not an excuse for treating you the way he did," I said. We walked into the bed and breakfast, and I was instantly glad we had come. A large Christmas tree decorated with silver and blue ornaments stood tall in the corner. Garlands adorned the banister that led to the second floor, and holiday music poured through speakers.

This was how Christmas was supposed to be done. I just hated that we had to celebrate behind closed doors. I tried to tell myself that having Eli Hunt film his movie here was worth it, but I wasn't so sure it was anymore.

As we passed the front desk, I noticed Dottie sneak several of the wrapped mints from the front counter. She tried to do it without anyone noticing, but in her quest for stealth, she accidentally knocked the entire bowl to the floor.

"Oh, I'm so sorry," Dottie spluttered, trying to bend down low enough to help clean them up.

Skittles immediately seized the opportunity, knowing she had a limited time for fun before it was taken away from her. She leaped forward, tearing the leash out of Autumn's grasp, and batted the candies, sending several of them skittering across the tile floor. It looked like she was playing her own version of air hockey as she sped across the floor to capture the rouge mints.

"Sorry, I let go of the leash when she jumped forward because I didn't want her to get hurt," Autumn said, watching helplessly as Skittles took another shot at the mints.

Leanne squatted and swept the remaining spilled mints into the bowl with one fluid motion, before placing it back on the counter. "No problem. I really need to find a better place for that thing. It's knocked off the counter at least two times a day. And that's during our slow season. With a full house like we have right now? It's hourly."

I didn't know if that was true or if Leanne was saying it to make Dottie feel better, but it did the trick. My sister smiled and unwrapped one of the mints she'd pocketed. "Well, they're good mints. Better than those strawberry candies you used to have."

I grimaced at the comment, reminded of the role those candies had played in a murder investigation just last year.

Leanne laughed. "I think the only person who enjoyed those was my mother." She turned toward the dining room as Autumn scooped the cat into her arms and held her tight. "Since you brought Skittles, I'm assuming you're here for enchiladas and tuna."

That, among other things, like information on who had died.

"Right you are," Dottie said.

Leanne glanced back at us as she walked. "Unfortunately for you, it's quite busy today. I have the entire film crew here because filming has been postponed temporarily while the sheriff investigates the explosion. It sounds like they'll be able to resume filming in the next hour, so they are all in a hurry to get fed. I hope you don't mind a wait."

"Not at all," I said, trying to hide how surprised I was that it was still business as usual, considering what had happened that morning. Disappointment that I couldn't be on set today settled in my chest. I'd already promised Dottie I wouldn't go, but part of me was tempted to anyway.

And then I thought of Dottie and how scared she'd been for me. No, it was good that I was home with her today.

"You don't happen to know who it was that died in the explosion, do you?" I asked.

Leanne shook her head and then motioned for us to follow her. "There's a lot of conflicting information going around, but it was someone connected to the movie. No one from town."

I tried to mask my relief. Any death was a tragedy, but there was a sense of comfort in it being a stranger. I didn't know if that made me a bad person or if it was simply human nature.

And if Leanne didn't know who it had been, that must mean it hadn't been Eli Hunt. That news would have been too big to contain.

We entered the dining room, and I was taken aback by how many people were there. When Leanne had said the entire film crew was on their lunchbreak, I hadn't realized the magnitude of that statement. Almost every table was filled with young people, and their collective conversations were almost deafening. There would be no eavesdropping today—I could barely hear myself think.

"Are we okay to have Skittles here?" I asked. "Usually when we bring her, it's during the off-season and your restaurant is empty. I'd hate to spoil anyone's lunch with an allergic reaction. Or at the very least, cat hair."

Leanne hesitated, like the thought hadn't even crossed her mind. "That's a good point. Maybe eat out on the patio? We closed it up for winter, but it's a beautiful day, and I don't mind prepping a table out there for you."

"That sounds perfect," Dottie said, her words quick. She didn't love crowds, and eating inside with all this chaos would be torture.

As we moved through the crowded dining room, however, Skittles had other plans. When we paused to wait for a group of young men to pass in front of us, Skittles took full advantage of the moment. She leaped out of Autumn's arms and ran toward a table that had just been vacated, judging by all the dirty plates on it.

"Skittles," Autumn shrieked, even as the cat jumped onto the table and helped herself to someone's leftovers. Autumn hurried over and grabbed both Skittles and the leash. "I'm sorry, Leanne. I can't seem to contain her today."

Leanne only laughed. "With Skittles, I'm used to it by now."

Autumn glanced at the other guests, seeming worried what reaction they might have to the cat helping itself to whatever food it could find.

She needn't have worried. No one even noticed the cat, too absorbed in their own food and conversation.

Leanne unlocked a set of glass doors on the far side of the room and led us outside to a dusty table. "I'll send someone over with a washcloth and a can of tuna, as well as your drinks." She glanced between us, then guessed, "Three waters?"

She'd already known Dottie and I only ever ordered water, but she looked at Autumn.

"Water is good for me," Autumn said.

Leanne released a sigh of relief, as if anything more than a water might have done her in, then hurried away, leaving us alone.

"No one here seems worried about the explosion," I said, settling into my chair. I could only see one table through the open doors, but three men were laughing at a shared joke while eating their enchiladas and drinking their sodas. "I can't believe they are going to return to work today, considering what happened. Are accidents such a common occurrence in the film industry that they can just carry on?"

Autumn raised a shoulder. "There's that saying, 'The show must go on.'"

I'd always figured that referred to live plays, where the main actors had understudies in case they got sick, but I supposed films had obligations and deadlines too.

Two men and a woman walked out the patio doors and moved to a table in a far corner, apparently not noticing the inch-thick layer of dust on it.

The woman looked familiar, and I had to do a double-take before realizing it was Jennifer, the production assistant. She glanced around nervously, as if making sure they were alone. Her gaze landed on me, and I smiled, giving her a small nod. She attempted a smile of her own, but it was forced, and she returned her attention to her two companions.

When our waitress, Jules, came out to wash off our table, she seemed surprised there was another occupied table. She hid her surprise like the hospitality expert she was, and, after giving Skittles her tuna, walked over to Jennifer's table, quickly wiping it down and then taking their orders.

When she'd finished, Jules returned to us and gave us an apologetic smile. "I hope you don't mind me helping them first," she said, her voice low, "but I don't know what kind of customers they are, and at least with you, I know you won't bite my head off if it takes twenty minutes to get your food out."

The poor woman seemed flustered, and I patted her

arm. "You do what you need to do to keep your guests happy," I said. "We're happy to wait."

The three of us ordered enchiladas while Skittles polished off her own meal, and then Jules once again sped away.

I knew I'd said I could wait as long as needed, but my stomach had a different opinion, and it gurgled and garbled. I sipped my water, hoping it would be enough to calm my stomach, and as I did so, I watched Jennifer and her two friends.

Jennifer and the two men were hunched forward, speaking in hushed tones. When Jules brought their food, which was much quicker than expected, giving me hope for my own food, they all stopped talking and waited until she left to resume their conversation.

I was intrigued. The only reason Dottie, Autumn, and I were eating outside was because of Skittles—so why were they? They had to have noticed that the tables hadn't been prepared for guests. They weren't clean, and the chairs had dirt and leaves all over them. Anyone else would have realized their mistake and returned inside.

"I think Skittles needs to stretch her legs," I said, standing suddenly. Dottie and Autumn gave me funny looks, probably because Skittles had walked to the bed and breakfast, and then had been running around and getting into trouble ever since we'd arrived. Her legs had had more than enough stretching.

That, and when I searched for the cat, I realized Skittles was curled up at Autumn's feet, half asleep, her leash coiled on the ground next to her.

"I'm not sure she agrees," Dottie said.

I didn't understand that cat. One minute she was jumping on tables and eating people's food like she owned the place, and the next she looked half dead, like she wouldn't be able to get up to save her own life.

I was sure it was a power play on her part.

"Of course she does," I said, picking up the leash and pulling on it.

Skittles lazily opened one eye, looking annoyed that I dared disturb her slumber, but didn't move to stand.

"See?" Dottie said, folding her arms with a smug smile.

I gave another firm pull, and Skittles grudgingly got to her feet, releasing a loud yawn followed by a long stretch.

"She was just preparing herself," I said. And then, before Dottie could say more, I walked Skittles over to the table of Jennifer and her two friends. I supposed I could have tried to make it look more natural, walk around a bit first, but it was an enclosed patio. There weren't exactly a lot of places to go.

The whispering trio immediately quieted. Jennifer pushed food around her plate while the men drank their sodas, apparently thinking that if they ignored me, I might go away.

There was a fourth seat at the table, and I swept some of the leaves off before plopping myself down on it, making myself at home.

"I see that you enjoy a beautiful afternoon as much as I do," I said, my voice bright. "Leanne opened up the patio for us to eat out here because Skittles gets antsy around large groups, and I've never seen so many people here at once."

The trio remained silent, exchanging looks that read, *How do we get rid of her?*

"You know her, don't you?" I continued. "Leanne Warner. She owns the bed and breakfast, but she also wrote the screenplay for *Amaretto*. She's talented in so many ways." I tried to keep my tone as cheerful as I could manage without also coming across like a crazy person, but judging by their expressions, I had failed on that count. Or maybe they had seen us inside and noticed that Skittles hadn't been at all antsy but had instead been happy to help everyone with their leftover food. Eating outside was a downgrade for her.

"Who are you again?" one of the men asked. He had a sharp nose and defined eyebrows that gave him the appearance of always being angry.

"I'm sorry. How rude of me," I said, holding out a hand. "Jo Darby. My sister and I own Sandcastle Bakery, and today was supposed to be my debut as a background actor. That's how I know Jennifer." I paused when the man didn't immediately take my hand. "And you are?"

"Pleased to make your acquaintance," the man said, though he didn't seem pleased at all. He did give my hand a quick shake, though it was probably an attempt to get me to lower it. His friend appeared to be the complete opposite of him, with blond hair and freckles. He looked like he wanted to make his own introduction but was given a look that stopped him before he could.

Jennifer glanced under the table, where Skittles was licking up something that had spilled on the patio.

"She's pretty. You said her name is Skittles?"

I nodded, my gaze still on the men. What was Jennifer doing hanging around guys like these?

"Yes," I said, my attention shifting to her. "My sister named her. If it had been up to me, I would have gone with something sneaky like Houdini because she's always getting into mischief. Fun fact, Harry Houdini actually worked in espionage, and it's no wonder the CIA chose him. I can't think of a better candidate."

Now I had the two men's interest.

"Was he really?" the blond man asked, his lips turned down in suspicion, like he didn't believe me.

I gave him a guilty smile. "Well, maybe. It's a theory. But what I can confirm is that many of his escape techniques were used by CIA agents as well as influenced spy gadgetry during the Cold War. The man was a genius. All that to say that Skittles, who will now be known as Houdini, is currently trying to drink what's left of your soda, and you should probably ask for another." I paused. "You aren't allergic, are you?"

The blond man seemed taken aback that there was, in fact, a cat now sitting on the table in front of him, enjoying his drink. "I'm not allergic," he said, and then he looked under the table, probably trying to figure out how she'd gotten up there without him noticing.

"She's very fast, isn't she," I said.

"Yes. Very." The blond looked more impressed than annoyed by it.

I turned to Jennifer. "I wanted to talk to you about this morning. I'm sorry I left without telling you. Patty said she wanted me home, resting, all because I had a bit of a tumble on the shuttle. When we heard the explosion, the only thing I could think of was to drop to the floor, and I dropped a bit harder than I'd intended. And then my sister showed up in a panic and—" I paused and then let my voice wobble a bit. "Everywhere I've gone today, I expect something to blow up. It's taken quite the toll on my nerves."

Jennifer rested a hand on mine. "It was scary," she said, her voice kind. "But you don't have anything to worry about. It was a one-time occurrence. I heard that it had something to do with a leak in a propane line or something."

I sneaked a glance at Jennifer's friends, and they were sharing concerned looks. It didn't seem to be concern about the explosion, however, but like they were uncomfortable with the conversation.

"A leaking propane line doesn't just explode on its own, though," I said, lifting my head and looking at Jennifer. "There needs to be a spark of some kind, and Christopher wasn't even inside his RV." I paused. "Do you know the man who got caught in the explosion?"

Jennifer glanced at the two men, who quickly averted their gazes.

"One of the extras," she finally said, her attention returning to me. She said it as if it had been rehearsed. "I hadn't yet met him, but his name was Blake Sommer."

5

My heart constricted. "You're sure?"

Jennifer nodded slowly, her gaze studying me. "Yes. The sheriff asked me to confirm that Blake was attached to the film. Why? Did you know him?"

"I only met him once. He sat next to me as we waited for our turn to board the shuttle. He wasn't much of a talker, but he seemed to have warmed up to me by the time you called for us." I paused, thinking of that poor young man who had been in desperate need of a haircut. "He had driven several hours just so he could be in a movie with Eli Hunt. A big fan. Honestly, I can't believe that you'll be able to continue filming this afternoon after what happened."

Jennifer released a sigh and shook her head. "I know it seems callous. The thing is, a movie is complicated with a lot of moving parts, and it's difficult to just shut all that down. We're cooperating with the sheriff in every aspect we can, though. And we'll be having a vigil for Blake tonight."

That was fast.

"How did they confirm so quickly that it was Blake down at the beach?" I asked. "He must have been burned pretty badly, and no one here knew him."

The two men at the table began to look antsy, shifting in their seats, like they couldn't wait for me to leave. I had a feeling that if I pushed any harder, I might have a personal escort.

I met the blond's gaze, and I refused to look away.

"Blake's wallet was found among the debris," he said, before shoving a forkful of enchilada into his mouth.

"That doesn't prove anything," I said. "Loads of people lose their wallets at the beach. And if you think about it, it shouldn't have been possible for him to be down there in the first place."

"How do you figure?" Jennifer asked.

"Because the man was sitting right next to me, waiting to ride the shuttle so we could film our scene. He was there when you called for us to go outside, and the explosion happened maybe ten minutes later. Blake had been waiting for two hours, so why would he suddenly get the urge to drive himself down to the director's trailer? That's the only way he could have gotten there quickly enough, and even then, I'm shocked he was able to make it all that way. He had to have been going quite fast." When I was met with blank stares from the rest of the table, I shook my head in disbelief. "That doesn't seem strange to any of you?"

The sharp-nosed man studied me, his gaze intense. He had been quietly listening to everything, but when he spoke, the other two stilled.

"What concern is it to you?" he asked, his words slow. "Your sheriff is looking into it, isn't he? Whatever might have happened this morning, whatever reason Blake had for being down there by the director's trailer, it is your sheriff's responsibility to discover it."

These three knew something they didn't want to share with me, but I wasn't going to get it by repeatedly asking for it like an impatient toddler trying to wear down their mother.

"You're right," I finally said. "I suppose I feel a connection with Blake, considering I'm probably the last person to have spoken with him before he died. There's something powerful in that." I paused, then turned to the two men. "I'm sorry for interrupting your lunch like this. I should get back to my own table. It looks like our food has arrived."

The blond man gave a slight nod. "Enjoy your meal."

"I will, thank you." I started to stand, but then paused. "I'm sorry, I didn't catch your name."

His friend spoke up, his gaze as sharp as his nose. "Like he said, enjoy your meal."

Jennifer gave me an apologetic smile but didn't say anything more, only gave me a little wave in farewell.

"Come along, Skittles," I said, pulling on her leash. It seemed we'd overstayed our welcome.

I glanced back toward their table as we walked away, pretending I was checking to make sure the cat was following me, and immediately noticed the tension between the three companions. Jennifer's face was furrowed in either anger or frustration, I couldn't tell which, and her sharp-nosed friend was matching it. It seemed the blond was the referee of the group, but he wasn't doing a very good job of it.

Those three knew something they shouldn't...or they'd been involved in something they shouldn't. Considering their reaction to my interference, I suspected it was the latter.

I plopped down in my chair next to Dottie, letting go of Skittles' leash, and breathed in the aroma of my enchiladas. As important as that conversation had been, my stomach had taken over, and I dug into my food.

Dottie and Autumn watched me eat.

I swallowed a bite of food and looked between them. "What?"

"Nothing," Dottie said. "Only you're acting like you just pulled yourself out of the Sahara Desert and this is the first food you've seen in weeks." She then handed me a napkin and pointed to my chin.

I wiped the cheese that was hanging from it, then dove back in. "I'm hungry. Is that a crime?"

"It's not," Autumn said, "but considering the anxious

glances that other table is sending your way, you touched a nerve. With that in mind, when it's convenient, you should probably share what that nerve was and if we should be concerned."

Dottie snorted. "You're being too kind." She turned to me. "Jo, that enchilada isn't going anywhere. You need to tell us what just happened. I still have my cop's intuition, and something isn't right with those people."

"I agree," I said. "I like Jennifer, but I don't love that she's hanging out with those two guys—they're not good influences on her. It's so important to be careful when choosing your peer group."

"Tell us about Jennifer," Dottie said.

"She's the production assistant on the movie."

Both Dottie and Autumn gave me blank stares.

"You're the expert on movie sets. What does that mean?" Autumn prompted when I didn't explain further.

Expert. I liked the sound of that.

Dottie scowled at Autumn. "That's just what we needed —an overconfident Jo. There's no telling what she'll do now."

I smiled and ignored my sister. "Basically, anything that happens on set, it goes through Jennifer. Everything from ordering catered lunch for the actors to making sure the extras have the proper paperwork and assignments. If the director needs something, he asks her."

"And the two men?" Dottie asked.

I frowned. "I'm not sure. They refused to give me their

names, and the guy with the dark hair seems to be the leader of the group. When he spoke, everyone else got quiet, like they were scared of him." I glanced toward their table but saw it was empty. I turned to see them entering the bed and breakfast through the patio doors. I hadn't even noticed them walking by—I was losing my edge. I hoped they hadn't overheard anything.

"Do you think they know something about the explosion?" Autumn asked, lowering her voice. "Maybe it wasn't an accident and they know who did it." A year ago, Autumn would have wanted nothing to do with something like this, and now she was suggesting arson and murder—we'd had a bad influence on her.

"I honestly think it was a freak accident," I said, "which makes it even sadder for Blake."

"Blake?" Dottie asked, her gaze snapping to me.

I forgot I hadn't gotten that far.

"Blake Sommer. He was an extra I was sitting next to while waiting to go on set. He was the one who was killed in the explosion."

Autumn's eyes widened, and Dottie released a quick breath.

"You should have led with that," Dottie said.

Yes, I supposed I should have, but there were so many thoughts swirling through my head, it was difficult to know where to start.

"He was an out-of-towner, excited to finally meet one of his celebrity heroes, poor guy," I said. "What I don't understand is why he would have been down at the beach at all. He should have been on the shuttle with us, and yet he drove all the way down to the beach, just in time to be caught in that explosion. It's as if as soon as Jennifer announced that we'd be driving to set, he helped me out of my chair and then hurried down there."

"We can't always know what's going on in someone's mind," Dottie said. "And unless he shared his intentions with someone else, we may never know." Her voice was sad, and I wondered if coming to the bed and breakfast was helping Dottie feel better or only making things worse. She'd had plenty of unsolved cases just like this, where there were far too many questions and never enough answers.

"Maybe he did share his intentions," I said, thinking back to who had been sitting near me in that waiting area. If anyone else had spoken to Blake, it would have been Dr. Patty.

"You okay with us taking the scenic route home?" I asked, scooting my chair back. It scraped across the cement, and Dottie and Autumn both winced, covering their ears.

"As long as you promise to not do that again," Autumn said.

Fair enough.

Dottie wasn't so willing to blindly agree. "And where exactly would we be going?"

I hesitated to tell her. Dottie not only avoided doctor

appointments, she also avoided Dr. Patty in general. My sister couldn't come to terms with growing old, and Patty never minced words about the reality of it. Dottie thought the doctor should mind her own business.

My experience with Patty had been quite the opposite —she'd given me wonderful advice on how I could improve my health and feel better. Dottie refused to listen, though, and instead relied on the folk wisdom of our departed mother. If it was good enough for her, it was good enough for us.

This was the same mother who had insisted that exposure to cold weather would cause us to catch a cold and that an apple a day kept the doctor away.

Even now, Dottie never went outside if the temperature was below forty degrees. And she still ate more apples than I thought was good for her. So. Many. Apples.

After paying for our meal, rather than walking back through the bed and breakfast, we left via a side gate that led from the enclosed patio to a meditation garden. A path led us back around the building and onto the main road.

"Where did you say we are going?" Dottie asked, pausing to catch her breath and give Skittles a scratch behind the ear.

She knew I had never said where, but it was cute that my sister thought she could trip me up like that.

"There were a lot of people waiting with me at the community center," I said brightly. "I doubt I was the only one who spoke to Blake." I hoped Dottie would let it go at that.

She didn't.

"And the first one we'll be visiting is..." She waited for me to finish her sentence.

"Just on the next street over." And then I pushed forward in an attempt to speed-walk. It was more of a shuffle, and I couldn't keep it up for long, but it was enough that I put a solid eight feet between us.

As soon as we turned the corner at the bottom of the road, though, and Dottie saw the sign for the health clinic, she knew.

"No. Absolutely not."

She didn't have the chance to turn around because Sheriff Hart called to us from across the street. He'd been walking in the opposite direction but immediately beelined toward us.

"Jo and Dottie, just the women I was looking for."

6

It was never a good sign when the sheriff was looking for you.

"Let me guess," I said with a smile. "You were in the mood for some pastries and were devastated when you saw that we'd closed up shop. We'd be more than happy to open back up for you—anything to keep our local law enforcement happy and well fed."

The sheriff's lips twitched up, as if he wanted to smile but couldn't quite bring himself to do it.

"I wish that was my biggest problem today," he said, instead releasing a long sigh. "Jo, I have it on good authority that you were the last person who spoke to our victim."

That hadn't taken long.

"Oh, dear. I'd hoped it wouldn't be someone I knew," I

KAT BELLEMORE

said, deciding that playing dumb was the best strategy here. "Are you allowed to tell me who it was?"

My acting skills weren't what they should have been and Sheriff Hart bent his head, shaking it. "You already heard, huh?"

I hesitated, then nodded. "Word travels fast around here, but you already know that. I'm assuming you talked to Patty about me." The woman might be a wonderful doctor, but she also was an insatiable gossip. I actually admired the quality.

His lips twitched up again. "I did."

"We were actually just stopping by to see her."

I was a little disappointed that he'd beat us to it but also pleased, weirdly enough. Small-town sheriffs tended to get a bad rap, but I liked Sheriff Hart and thought he was quite good at his job.

Unlike me, Sheriff Hart was not pleased.

His lips pursed, and I realized my mistake—he thought we were interfering with his investigation. Which we weren't—not really. We were curious about why Blake had been on the beach, that was all.

I hurriedly added, "I've been having these heart palpitations ever since the explosion this morning, and I'm sure it's just anxiety, but I wanted her to give a listen. Just in case."

The sheriff nodded, but I could tell he didn't believe me. And that was good. After everything the sheriff and I had been through, I'd hoped he'd learned by now that I had an excuse for everything, and those excuses were especially good when I was doing something I shouldn't.

That made me sound like a bad person, but I only ever lied to him when it was for the greater good. And understanding why Blake had rushed down to the director's trailer when he should have been on the shuttle with the rest of us was for the greater good. Blake had been a nice kid who had helped me when I'd needed it, and he deserved justice, in whatever form that took. Even if it was just a deeper understanding of what had happened today.

"Do you not think I'm capable of doing my job?" Sheriff Hart asked, looking more tired than he had five minutes ago.

"Oh, no, of course you are," I said, appalled that that had been what he'd taken from my comment. "And I would never want you to think otherwise. You are observant and fair and—"

Sheriff Hart held up a hand, stopping me. "Then why do you never let me do it? It undermines my efforts if you're running around town talking to people."

"Oh, you know that's not true," Autumn said, lifting her chin in defiance. "It's never undermined you. In fact, Jo has been quite helpful."

My heart swelled. Autumn was terrified of the sheriff, which was understandable, considering she had been a suspect in a murder a couple of years earlier.

So, her standing up for me right now—it was a big deal.

"Thank you, Autumn," I said, "but the sheriff is right."

Dottie and Autumn looked at me as if I were a strange creature from an alien planet, and Sheriff Hart tilted his head, like he thought he'd heard me wrong.

"Sorry?" he said, looking confused.

"You're right," I repeated. "Dottie is constantly telling me that there is nothing worse than a civilian who thinks they can do a cop's job better than they can. People get hurt. I don't want to be that person." When everyone continued to stare, apparently still too stunned to speak, I continued. "Besides, there's no foul play here, right? Even though Blake was a lovely young man, it was a case of being in the wrong place at the wrong time. It's tragic, but it's not like you're going to be arresting anyone for it. Me trying to find a problem where there isn't one—that would only create a new problem, and no one wants that."

And that was when I got what I was looking for. The brief flash of guilt that always crossed the sheriff's face when he was about to hide something from me.

He didn't feel guilty about not sharing information with me—his opinion was strong on that point. But it felt dishonest to him—felt like lying. And he hated it.

On the other hand, Sheriff Hart knew that hiding information from me was the only way for me to not become involved.

Unfortunately for him, I already was involved. I was the last person to see Blake alive.

"It was an accident, wasn't it?" I said.

Rather than answer me, Sheriff Hart moved his gaze to something else in the distance, as if in deep thought. Eventually his gaze returned to me—once he'd removed all emotion from his expression.

"I hope you really have embraced this new way of thinking—this new philosophy," he said. "The last thing I want to see is you in trouble, Jo."

That last statement—it was sincere. He really did want the best for me, and I loved him for it. It almost made me feel bad for what I was about to do.

"I understand there is going to be a vigil for Blake this evening," I said. "I'm sure you have all of Blake's belongings locked up while you finish up your investigation, but do you think you could release Blake's car long enough to have it there? I don't know anything about cars, but the way he talked about it—it was important to him."

The sheriff glanced at Dottie and Autumn, as if they would have any idea what I was talking about, but they merely shrugged.

"What car?" he asked slowly. I could tell he didn't want to encourage me, but he needed to know what I was talking about, and that need trumped everything else.

"I don't remember the name of it, but I do know it was yellow with black stripes." I tapped my chin, as if that would help me come up with anything useful. "It might have been a racing car. Anyway, I'm assuming it was parked down at the beach when the accident occurred, because I saw Blake only ten minutes before the explosion.

Driving is the only way Blake could have gotten down there that fast."

The sheriff's reaction told me everything. There had not been a yellow car with black stripes down at the beach, which meant that Blake had not driven himself there. Someone else had to have been behind the wheel.

Whether the sheriff liked it or not, there was more to this 'accident' than he wanted to admit, and I could be helpful.

Sheriff Hart held up a finger, indicating he needed a minute, and then he stepped away to make a phone call.

"You must be on to something because he does not look happy," Dottie whispered. "Too bad too, because you just made that great speech about how you getting involved only creates more problems."

I smiled. "Did you believe it when I said that?"

She gave me a skeptical eye. "Yes."

"Good, then that means so did he."

Autumn laughed at Dottie's stunned expression. "Jo can't be anyone other than who she is, so you might as well protect her—because heaven knows there's no use trying to stop her."

Dottie shook her head and muttered, "Don't I know it."

"Glad to see that's settled," I said with a satisfied nod.

The sheriff ended his call, then turned to us. He was silent, as if calculating what he might say next. He must have thought better of it because he turned away and began walking in the opposite direction.

"Sheriff Hart, that was about the car, wasn't it," I said, trying to catch up but struggling to walk fast enough. "I'm the one who told you about it. Can't you at least confirm or deny?"

The sheriff paused only long enough to glance over his shoulder and say, "Yes, it was about the car." And then he hurried away faster than I could ever hope to go.

I stopped and frowned. "Well, that wasn't very nice."

"You expected him to react any differently?" Dottie asked. "He knows you, and the more time he spends with you, the further you'll insert yourself into the investigation."

"Well, the joke's on him because ignoring me only encourages me to ask more questions." I folded my arms over my chest, thinking. "I don't think Blake knew anyone in town, and yet someone drove him down to the beach, more specifically, to the director's trailer."

"Which then blew up," Autumn said.

My gaze snapped to Dottie. "Not only was that explosion intentional, but I think that Blake Sommer was supposed to die."

7

I knew it sounded crazy, and judging by Dottie's dubious expression, she felt similarly, but I knew I was right. Blake Sommer was supposed to die.

But why?

"He was just an extra," I murmured. "He was inconsequential, driving three hours so he could get his hundred bucks and a chance at being on the big screen. Nothing more."

Both Dottie and Autumn raised an eyebrow as I continued to mutter to myself.

"You okay?" Dottie asked.

I started to nod, but it morphed into a shake of the head. "Blake wasn't from Starlight Ridge, and it doesn't seem that anyone connected with the movie knew him personally. Why would someone go out of their way to kill him?"

A voice spoke up from behind me. "Might have something to do with that text he received."

I turned to see Patty standing in the doorway of the medical clinic, leaning against the doorframe.

She smiled and walked over to us. "Sorry to interrupt, but I saw you out here talking with the sheriff, and when you didn't leave right way, I thought I'd see what was up."

I would have done the same thing.

"What text?" Dottie asked.

"That extra you were talking to while we were waiting earlier today, Blake—he received a text just after Jennifer instructed us to head out to the shuttle." She glanced at me. "It must have spooked him because he pushed past everyone in his rush to get outside."

"You don't know what happened after that?" I asked.

She shook her head. "Nope. My back was hurting, and I was just happy to have an excuse to stand up and move around a little bit."

It seemed that even doctors weren't immune to the effects of aging.

"Well, thanks anyway, Patty. That was helpful."

We turned to leave, but the doctor called out to us once more.

"Don't you want to know what I told the sheriff when he questioned me?"

All three of us immediately stopped and turned back. Skittles wasn't thrilled about the delay—she was in exploratory mode, and she pulled on the leash in an attempt to keep Autumn walking.

"There was something else?" I asked.

Patty smiled, loving the attention. "You know how when we first arrived at the community center, we had to fill out the paperwork and check in with wardrobe and all that? Well, Blake was with me for the entire process."

When she didn't continue, I prompted her. "And did he do anything out of the ordinary?"

"It didn't seem like it at the time," Patty said. "But when he was filling out the paperwork, he had a hard time answering even the most basic questions. He couldn't give the production team an address because he had just moved, couldn't remember his social security number, and he had to look at his phone to write down his cell number. I understand a teenager not knowing that stuff, but this guy was an adult. At some point you need to start acting like it."

That was interesting, especially for a guy who had given me such a detailed description about the car he drove.

"Thanks, Patty," I said. "We appreciate it. You know how the sheriff is—he gets a bit protective about his investigations."

"As he should," Dottie added.

I held back an eye roll and smiled—it was bigger than what was natural, and I hoped Dottie noticed the sarcasm behind it. "Of course he should."

As we walked away, Autumn asked, "What do you think?"

I knew exactly what I thought—that Blake wasn't who he had claimed to be, and he hadn't been in Starlight Ridge for the reasons he'd professed. The thought made me sad because I really had liked Blake.

For now, I'd keep those thoughts to myself. I didn't want to speak ill of the dead without proof to back it up—once you spoke something out loud, it could never be taken back, and I didn't want to do that to Blake. Not yet, anyway.

"What I think," I said slowly, "is that I'm ready for an afternoon nap. It's been a trying day."

I wasn't lying. I really did need to rest. Because if I was going to get any useful information out of the vigil later that evening, I was going to need to be at my best.

I didn't know if Blake was who he'd said he was, but if he had been lured to his death, his murderer was likely going to be at the vigil. And I didn't want to miss a thing.

"WHY COULDN'T they have waited to have this in the morning?" Dottie grumbled as we walked in the dark toward the boardwalk.

"Because everyone wants candles at a vigil, Dottie, and you can't have candles at ten in the morning."

As we drew closer, I saw that several tables had been set up. I didn't know what they were all for, though, because there were no pictures. There were, however, several news crews.

"How much do you want to bet that the movie production team wanted to have the vigil quickly, hoping that the media wouldn't find out about Blake's death?" Autumn asked, her hands shoved in her pockets in an attempt to warm them. "A background actor dying in an explosion can't be good publicity, and as far as anyone knows, it could have been negligence. This is Eli Hunt's first time as a producer, and it's going to be clouded with conspiracy theories."

"Well, if they didn't want the media to find out about it, they failed pretty spectacularly," I said, taking in all the cameras before glancing at Autumn. "You know a lot about how this all works."

She laughed and shook her head. "No, I just read the gossip magazines at the salon when I'm getting my hair cut, and it makes me think I know something."

"I don't think you're wrong, though," Dottie said, taking in the scene. "No one here actually knew Blake. His family will have been notified, but they probably didn't have enough time to get here for the vigil. Blake lived three hours away, and who knows where his family lives."

"So, it's all for show," I said. The thought saddened me. A life had been taken, and instead of celebrating that life and mourning the early departure of it, people were trying to make it all go away. After today, these people didn't want to ever have to think about Blake Sommer again.

And there, right in the middle of all the cameras, near the table that held candles, was Eli Hunt. He looked different than in the movies—shorter. But just as handsome. Maybe even more so. I tried to keep myself from fangirling, reminding myself that we were here to pay our respects to Blake.

"Let's get ourselves a candle," I said, moving in his direction. "It won't look right if we don't."

We had to maneuver around the cameras to reach the table, and when we did, I heard Eli being asked questions he shouldn't have been expected to know the answers to.

"What can you tell us about Blake Sommer and his role in *Amaretto*?" one of the reporters asked.

Eli's gaze dropped, and in a British accent, he responded. "His role, same as the role of all our background actors, was as important to the film as mine is. Without background actors, comedy films would look post-apocalyptic." He paused. "Blake Sommer had an infectious laugh and an amazing work ethic, and he will certainly be missed."

I snorted. He would be missed? That was the thing with background actors. They were replaceable. Eli Hunt hadn't known Blake, and he wouldn't think of him again after tonight.

Eli heard my snort and shot me a side glance, his obvious annoyance fading when he saw it just an old woman.

"Has the explosion been ruled an accident?" another reporter asked.

"That's a good question for the sheriff," Eli responded. "As far as my understanding, yes, it was an accident. Blake was meant to be in a scene that we were preparing to film on the beach."

Another reporter: "Do you think Blake's family is going to sue you for the incident that occurred today?"

It was obvious that this was a question Eli had no intention of answering, and he raised a hand. "Thank you so much for coming out and helping us celebrate Blake's life." He then turned his back on the reporters and picked up two candles. He surprised me by handing them to Dottie and me. Looked like the movie star had been relegated to candle duty.

Jennifer appeared out of the dark to our left and directed the reporters to a lighting ceremony that was about to begin, where participants could send lighted lanterns into the sky, symbolic of Blake's ascension to Heaven.

Seemed a bit over the top to me, but I supposed that was what we got when Hollywood was in charge of a vigil.

"That was a nice tribute," I said to Eli as he picked up a third candle and handed it to Autumn. "You two must have been close."

He looked confused. "Hmmm?"

"Your tribute to Blake Sommer."

The actor opened his mouth, like he had been caught

in a lie and couldn't remember how the rest of the story went. Eventually, he just shook his head. "Oh. No, I didn't know the man." His British accent was deep and rich, but something felt off about it.

"Then how did you know about his infectious laugh or his work ethic?" I asked.

He looked guilty and gave a small laugh. "I had to say something to keep the reporters at bay. You understand."

Seriously, there was something going on with that accent.

"Are you British?" I asked, catching him off guard as I abruptly changed the subject.

He hesitated. "For all intents and purposes, yes."

"That's a no," Dottie said from beside me.

"But then why—" And then I remembered what Jennifer had told me. "That's right, you're a method actor. Which means that during the filming of this movie, you are from England. But you aren't really. And your character wouldn't be speaking with reporters at a vigil for a background actor that he didn't know. So, how do you reconcile the two?"

Eli looked like he was losing patience with my questions. He'd needed to put on a good show for the reporters, but he didn't with me.

"I act as if my character were at a vigil. If he were here, what would he do?"

I thought about the scene we'd be shooting in a couple

of weeks—the one where I was supposed to pretend I liked going to bars.

"You'd be drunk," I said. "You'd be completely disrespectful and you'd crash it, wouldn't you? Leanne Warner is a friend of mine, and she told me that *Amaretto* is a movie about a drunk Englishman who wears far too much leather and falls for a woman who owns a small chocolate shop. Love wins, and he changes his ways. A tale as old as time."

Eli Hunt studied me. He was indeed wearing a leather jacket, so that tracked, and he had far too much gel in his dark hair. He looked like a wannabe Elvis Presley, if Elvis had facial hair. The movie star had just enough scruff to make him look both rugged and handsome.

"There are limits to what I do," Eli finally said. "Would my character have shown up drunk? Maybe. But he's a complex person who hasn't completely lost his humanity. There is still hope for him, and I'd like to think that he would have had the decency to show some respect for the dead."

That was a surprising answer, and a good one. Maybe there was hope for the real Eli Hunt, as well. Rumor had it that he was in the midst of a terrible divorce, or at least that was what Autumn had told me, and I couldn't imagine how difficult it must be to walk the line between the real world and this world he'd created for himself.

"Very well put," I told him, then stuck out my hand. "My name is Jo Darby, and I'm a big fan of yours. This is my sister Dottie and our friend Autumn. We own a French bakery around the corner, and Autumn is our pastry chef."

Eli took my hand. "Hello, Jo. Dottie. Autumn. It's nice to meet you."

Autumn looked like she might faint when he said her name, and I bit back a smile.

"I'm sorry I was a bit hard on you earlier," I told him, "but I'm also a background actor in your movie, and I was one of the last people to speak with Blake before he died. I didn't know him well, but he didn't seem the type to want to be paraded in front of news cameras or have a hundred lanterns sent up in his honor. He was more reserved than that."

Eli looked like he wanted to say something, but I rushed on. "I act like I knew Blake, but I didn't. And, well, frankly, this all feels a bit rushed for my liking, and I feel Blake deserved for his family to be here. People who cared for him and really knew him—people who could tell funny anecdotes or share the obstacles he overcame in his life. Maybe then we'd have gotten to know him, just a little, before saying goodbye."

Eli's expression fell as he took in the scene. There was one picture I hadn't noticed on a small table. It was a head-shot, probably the one that Blake had submitted with his application to be an extra on the film.

"It was too rushed for my liking too," Eli said, rubbing a hand over his face. "Despite what you might believe, I do wish we could have done things properly."

This time, Dottie was the one to snort. "You didn't want the media coverage is what it was—this looks bad for you. And you got the coverage anyway."

Eli didn't deny it, merely raising a shoulder. "No one likes the media horning in on this kind of thing. They sensationalize everything and frame things in whatever way will make them the most money."

"And in what way do you expect them to frame Blake's death?" Autumn asked.

Eli must have realized he'd said more than he'd intended because he immediately looked like he regretted speaking with us. "I'm sorry, I have obligations I need to attend to." And then he abruptly turned and struck up a conversation with the first person he saw—an older gentleman who looked like he had no idea who Eli Hunt even was.

"Don't mind him," a man said from behind us. "He doesn't want anyone to know the truth."

I turned to see the world-famous screenwriter Frederick Alberheist lighting up a cigarette. Or at least trying. It was a cheap lighter you'd get at a gas station, and he seemed to be having trouble with it. Eventually he gave up and snapped the lighter shut, slipping it into his pocket. I tried to mask my shock at seeing him still in Starlight Ridge. I'd thought he'd left when Leanne had kicked him out of the bed and breakfast, but I supposed I should have expected that a man like Frederick wouldn't go quietly.

Dottie and Autumn were having similar trouble hiding

their surprise, but at least Dottie was able to compose herself enough to respond.

"And what is the truth?" she asked, but in a tone that told me it didn't matter what Frederick said, she wasn't going to believe a word of it.

"That Eli Hunt knew Blake Sommer. Very well, in fact. And things between the two did not end well." Frederick paused. "Of course, this was nearly twenty years ago, so maybe Eli has forgotten. It's hard to imagine, though."

And then Frederick wandered away, twirling his unlit cigarette, like he'd forgotten why he was even there.

Like he hadn't just told us that Eli Hunt had lied to us.

Mistakes could happen—heaven knew my mind failed me more than I was comfortable with—but if what Frederick had said was true, whatever had happened between Blake Sommer and Eli Hunt wouldn't have easily slipped the movie star's memory.

That was the real question, though, wasn't it.

Could Frederick be trusted to tell the truth?

I didn't think so. But I'd been wrong before.

8

The three of us watched Frederick wander away, and I found myself questioning every conversation I'd had that day.

"We can't trust that man, right?" Autumn finally asked.

Dottie shook her head. "Definitely not. You saw how he acted at the bed and breakfast. He's completely off his rocker."

"And yet," I said, "what if it's true? What if Eli Hunt really did know Blake? If things didn't end well between the two, that would give Blake reason enough to drive out here and confront him. Maybe he threatened to go to the press and was demanding money for his silence. Or maybe he simply wanted an apology."

"You're assuming that Eli was the one who was in the wrong," Autumn pointed out. "If any of this is actually true."

That was a good point. Why had I automatically assumed that Eli had been to blame? Probably because he was the one in a position of power. Of course, he wouldn't have been twenty years ago. Eli had likely been at the very beginning of his acting career.

"Even if Blake came here to confront Eli, we don't actually think that Eli killed him, do we?" I asked, unable to imagine the actor doing something as violent as that. He might be a bit on the unconventional side, but he wasn't a murderer.

Of course, I had come across several murderers in the past who hadn't seemed the type. You never could tell.

"No, of course not," Autumn said, doubt tinging her voice. She didn't want to believe the movie star was capable of such a thing either, but, like me, she couldn't be sure.

"It depends on what it was that happened between the two," Dottie said in her no-nonsense way. "If it was something that could destroy Eli's career, he could be capable of anything. And if he could kill Blake, I hate to think what he'd do to three meddlesome women who stuck their noses where they didn't belong."

Meaning we should stop asking questions before we got ourselves blown up.

"So, what, we're going to just ignore everything we've heard and hope it will all work itself out somehow?" I asked. "Because you know that Frederick didn't tell the sheriff any of that stuff about Blake and Eli's past."

"How do you know he didn't?" Autumn asked. "Maybe he's telling anyone who will listen—anything to sabotage the movie. If he can't be a part of it—if he can't get credit where credit is due—then why wouldn't he?"

That was a good point. Frederick had a lot to gain by lying. Giving his lies credibility would only make things worse.

"Okay, so we don't follow up on it. Where does that leave us?"

"Nowhere," Dottie said. Her voice carried a lot of force, and it made both Autumn and me quiet down and listen. "There are some really powerful people here tonight. Eli Hunt, Frederick Alberheist, all those reporters... Don't underestimate the power of the media. They shape our worldview—everything from if you should neuter your pets to if our American troops should be involved in a conflict halfway around the world. Whether you like it or not, you rarely make a decision without the media having some kind of influence."

"And if one of those powerful people was involved in Blake's disappearance, you're saying they could come after us next," Autumn said, her voice small. She had finally started enjoying investigating mysteries with us, and now Dottie had scared her off.

I shook my head. "I'm sure that's not what she's—"

"Yes, it is," Dottie interrupted. "I was okay with asking questions when I thought it was something benign. I figured the explosion was due to a faulty refrigerator, like you suggested. These big corporations need to pay when they hurt their consumers. And let's be honest, we have no reason to believe that Blake's death wasn't an accident." She paused and pulled in a long breath. "But if it really was murder, and these are the people who are involved, I'm out. And you should be too."

My gaze moved over the vigil—the facade of doing something kind for a man who left the Earth too soon. When I examined people more closely, I saw them on their phones, wondering how long they needed to stay before it was appropriate to leave. I saw people sobbing when the cameras and reporters were paying attention to them, but their cheeks were dry as soon as the cameras panned away. Christopher stood to the side of the vigil with Jennifer, and I had no doubt they were discussing the plans for the scenes they would be shooting the next day.

"No," I said. "I'm not going to let them win this game they've created. I know these people are the coaches and the players and the refs and the scorekeepers. I know it's rigged. But Blake deserves better than this. He deserves for someone to care that he is gone—not merely pretending to care for the sake of some cameras."

Autumn lightly touched my arm. "I'm sure he has family that will give him a proper funeral and—"

"It's not enough," I said, anger welling in my chest. No wonder Adeline had been unhappy when she'd heard that Eli Hunt would be filming his next movie here, and even less happy when they'd approached her, asking to film inside her chocolate shop. She'd seen how toxic Hollywood could be, and now I was seeing it firsthand.

"What are you planning on doing?" Dottie asked, her tone wary. She had every right to be nervous. When I was passionate about something, I was unpredictable.

My gaze landed on the sheriff, who was helping himself to a plate of finger sandwiches. Without saying another word, because I was sure Dottie would try to stop me, I walked over to the sheriff.

"We need to talk," I said.

My sudden presence made him jump and nearly drop his food. When he saw it was me, he released a weary sigh. "Hello, Jo."

I eyed his plate. "That's a lot of food for one person. Are they not paying you enough as sheriff? I can make a few calls to make sure you're being treated properly. Or I can have Dottie call. They'd probably respond better to her."

"No need to do that. They're treating me well enough," the sheriff said. He had been reaching for another sandwich but changed his mind and pulled his arm back. "What can I do for you, Jo?"

"We need to speak in your office. It's urgent."

Sheriff Hart glanced at me, and he looked torn. I could tell he really didn't want to entertain whatever craziness I usually brought into his life, but I could also see the curiosity behind it. "It's important that I'm here at the vigil," he finally said.

"Yes, I know. You still have an active investigation, and you think your murderer is here tonight. I've read that it's not unusual for a murderer to return to the scene of the crime, attend the funeral, etcetera. But that's why I need to speak with you. It's about your investigation."

Sheriff Hart released another sigh. "Have you been getting involved, Jo? You said you wouldn't. You said it would cause more problems."

"I know I did. I'm sorry, but I had to say something to help you feel better. You were annoyed with me, and I don't like you being annoyed with me."

He took one last look around the vigil. "Make it quick." And then he started walking toward the sheriff's station.

Dottie and Autumn joined me as I followed him.

"What do you think you're doing?" Dottie whispered. "Are you trying to get yourself killed? Requesting to meet with the sheriff out in the open like this is asking for trouble. If Blake's death wasn't an accident, then every person who has motive to cover this thing up is undoubtedly watching you right now."

"Every person meaning Eli Hunt," I said. "As far as we know, there isn't anyone else who knew Blake."

"I guess," Dottie said. "But I don't doubt that there is more than one person here who might have liked to frame Eli."

"Frederick," I guessed. "He kills Blake and then spreads the rumor that Eli and Blake had history together. He says he wouldn't be surprised if Eli killed

Blake. The movie is destroyed and Frederick gets his vengeance."

"Exactly," Dottie said. "Let's just go home. Tomorrow, when every famous person who is in Starlight Ridge right now is busy working on their film, that's when you go see the sheriff. No prying eyes."

"Jo, you coming?" Sheriff Hart called to me.

I looked between him and Dottie.

"Sorry," I told her as I moved toward the sheriff's office. "I don't care who sees me. I need to do this."

Dottie didn't follow me as I'd expected her to. That was fine. I didn't blame her. This was a battle she was choosing not to fight. Still, I couldn't help but be disappointed. She had always been someone I could count on to have my back.

Sheriff Hart waited for me, then opened the station's door and held it, allowing me to enter first. He followed me in, set his plate of food down on the desk, then leaned against it, his arms folded across his chest. "All right, Jo. What's so urgent that it couldn't wait until morning?"

I pulled in a deep breath. "Frederick Alberheist approached me at the vigil. We had seen him earlier in the day at the bed and breakfast, arguing with Leanne. He wanted to be a part of the movie and potentially take credit for the screenplay Leanne had written, so she kicked him out. This evening, he started making accusations against Eli Hunt, saying that Eli and Blake Sommer had a history together and that things had ended badly. I'm not sure how the dots connect, but it's very possible that Frederick Alberheist is at the center of it."

Sheriff Hart nodded, mulling over the information. After a few moments of silence, his gaze met mine. "And why are you coming to me with this now? Usually you wait until it's a life-or-death situation, then ask me to step in and save the day."

I didn't think that was a fair assessment, until I really started thinking about it. The sheriff might have a point.

"I hear your feedback and I accept it," I said. "The thing is, Dottie is worried about my safety. She says these are powerful people and if I get too close to the truth, Blake may not be the only one to disappear. I don't know if she's right or not, but I do know that I don't believe the explosion was an accident. I believe Blake Sommer was lured to the trailer. It's the only thing that makes sense. Except, he didn't live here in Starlight Ridge. No one knew him, or so I thought."

Sheriff Hart raised a finger, stopping me from continuing. "I'll ask the question again. Why now?"

"Because no one else cares what happened to Blake," I said. "These film people put together a quick get-together to look like they care, but it's just for show, like everything else they do. No one cares—except for you. And I know that you and I have had our differences and I usually don't tell you anything because I know you'll try to stop me, but I couldn't just sit around and do nothing. If this information is helpful, I wanted you to have it."

Sheriff Hart was quiet for another moment as he studied me. "Would it help you to know that Blake Sommer had no family? His parents gave him up for adoption when he was a child, and he spent several years in foster care until he eventually ran away. If this was murder, solving it won't provide anyone closure."

No family. Poor Blake.

"Why would that help? That only makes it worse," I said.

Sheriff Hart nodded, like he'd expected as much. "Then what about this? What if I told you that Blake was not a good man? When he ran away from his foster home, they never even filed a missing person report. Since then, he's managed to get himself a long rap sheet that includes, among other things, multiple counts of possession and armed robbery."

A drug addict who had violent tendencies and stole from innocent people. That wasn't great.

"No, it doesn't help," I whispered.

Sheriff Hart gave me a kind smile. "I'm telling you this because I don't want you losing sleep over Blake Sommer. Not to say that his life wasn't worth something. No matter what his background was, he deserves justice to be served. And in many ways, I don't fault Blake for choosing the path he did. But I don't want you to feel like the weight of this investigation rests on your shoulders. You are not the only one who cares about knowing what really happened to this man."

"Thank you," I said.

"With that being said, Dottie is right. I believe at least one powerful and dangerous person is behind the explosion. And until I've made an arrest, for your own safety, you need to stay away."

"You would have said that even if powerful and dangerous people weren't involved," I said.

Sheriff Hart gave me a sad smile. "Powerful and dangerous people are always involved."

From my experience, that was very true.

I said goodnight, but as I moved to leave the office, I noticed the corner of an evidence bag peeking out from the sheriff's desk drawer.

"Sheriff Hart, before I leave, I wondered if you'd be so kind as to let me borrow your flashlight. It's gotten dark, and I'm not sure that Dottie and Autumn waited for me. I'd feel a lot safer if I had some light."

"Of course. I have some spares in the supply closet."

As he moved to the back of the station, I squatted as if to tie my shoe and opened the drawer. It was full of a variety of nicknacks and seemed to serve both as a lost and found and an evidence locker. I pushed aside car keys, a lighter, and a stuffed animal before lifting out the evidence bag.

My breath caught.

Inside the bag was a bullet casing.

Blake Sommer hadn't died in the explosion.

He'd been shot.

9

E quipped with the flashlight that the sheriff had so graciously lent me, I walked home, deep in thought. He'd known it was murder since that morning when he'd found the shell casing.

Who would hate Blake so much that they would shoot him? It was so much more personal than merely leading him into a trap.

Personal.

It didn't seem that Blake had many people in his life who could make things personal.

When I entered the back entrance to the bakery, I noticed the upstairs lights were off. It looked like Dottie had already gone to bed. After an arduous trek up the steep staircase, I unlocked the apartment door, ready to crawl under my own covers.

But the apartment—it was too quiet. Where was the soft rumble of Dottie's snoring?

"Dottie," I called.

No answer. I entered the hallway and was nearly to her bedroom when a shadow jumped across the room, and I yelped.

A meow.

"Skittles," I said, breathing heavily. "You can't do that to a person."

Another meow, and then she was rubbing against my leg. I picked her up and pushed Dottie's door open. Her bed was empty.

I wondered if she was still at the vigil. But why would she hang around there when she was the one who'd said we should be home?

"It looks like I have a sister to find," I told Skittles, placing her down on Dottie's bed. I glanced at the clock. Eight-thirty. I worried that Dottie had gotten so tired, she hadn't been able to finish the walk home.

I dreaded having to take the stairs again, but I reminded myself that it was good for me.

"One step. Two step. Red step. Blue step," I said to myself, trying to distract myself from the sheer steepness of the stairs. I chuckled—I was really funny sometimes.

When I reached the bottom of the staircase, it was a relief that I hadn't fallen down them. There was a silver lining in everything, if you looked hard enough.

But before I could go back outside to look for Dottie,

the door flew open and a dark shape stumbled inside—straight into me.

"I do parkour," I shouted as I fell backward and onto the floor.

"So what? It hasn't done you any good," Dottie answered from the dark as we tried to untangle ourselves. We gave up and lay on the floor, breathing heavily.

"Why weren't you home?" I asked when I had enough breath to do so. "I was preparing to come out and look for you."

"Look for me?" Dottie yelped, pushing herself into a seated position. "I waited for you at the vigil, and you never returned. I thought you'd been taken by Frederick, and I was coming back here to get my gun."

I used her to pull myself up. "How could I have known that you'd waited? The last thing you said to me was to go home."

"You thought I'd leave you on your own? Just because I couldn't support what you were doing didn't mean I was abandoning you."

As much as my sister drove me crazy sometimes, I sure loved her.

"Well, thank you for being willing to come after me with a gun," I said, grabbing onto the banister and pulling myself up. I held out a hand to Dottie and helped her do the same.

"And thank you for being willing to come out looking for me," Dottie said.

"Ready?" I asked.

She nodded. "Let's do this." And then we linked arms, resting opposite hands on the banisters that lined the staircase. In sync, like all sisters should, we climbed those stupid steps and went to bed.

I WAS JUST SITTING down to my bowl of cream of wheat when Dottie walked in, hair and makeup done, per her usual.

"Good morning," I said.

"Good morning," she said, even as she looked me up and down with a judgmental eye.

"What?"

Her gaze settled on my hair. "Nothing. It's only...this is the first time you've come to breakfast in your pajamas. And your hair looks like a small animal might live in it."

Our mother had instilled the strictest of standards for Dottie and me, and one of those was that the moment a woman awoke in the morning, she should dress in her best blouse and skirt, followed by fixing her hair and makeup. She should meet the day the same way she'd want to meet her future husband.

Of course, I didn't have one of those husbands in my future—I was a bit past my prime for all that—but the habits had remained. Somewhere along the way, I'd switched out the skirt for pants, but it was the principle that mattered.

Until today.

Today, I'd decided that nothing mattered.

"I don't want to go out today," I said.

Dottie nodded as she served herself a bowl of cream of wheat. "Okay, but what about the bakery? We'll have customers, I'm sure."

"They should accept me as I am," I said with a shrug.

Dottie stared for a moment before realizing the hot cereal was dripping down the side of the bowl and onto her finger. She quickly wiped it off and then joined me at the table. "Really, Jo, the dyed hair is one thing, but now you're not even going to try? What would Mother say?"

"We were blessed to have a mother that loved us. What does the rest matter?"

Dottie released a hard breath and shook her head. "This isn't like you. What happened last night with the sheriff?"

"Not much," I said. "It turns out that the murder of Blake Sommer is probably unsolvable, but lucky for us, it doesn't matter because no one will miss him." My voice held a bitterness that was unusual for me, but I didn't care.

Dottie blew on a spoonful of her cereal. "What do you mean, no one will miss him? What about his family?"

"Exactly as it sounds. It turns out that Blake's biological parents gave him up for adoption, and Blake's foster family couldn't care less if he was there or not. No one wanted him."

"Did he have any siblings?" Dottie asked. "Surely they would care."

"Maybe, but the sheriff didn't mention it, and, funnily enough, it didn't come up in my and Blake's brief conversation—you know, since I was a complete stranger who probably freaked him out. I do that—I start talking with strangers, trying to be all friendly like, but I see it in their eyes. They can't get away soon enough. It's probably similar to how Blake felt when his foster parents never came looking for him."

I knew I was spiraling, but I didn't know how to stop it. Last night had triggered something in me, and it had kept me awake all night. The things that had felt so important all my life now seemed inconsequential.

"That's really sad to hear about Blake," Dottie said, her voice softening. "But just because he didn't have a family doesn't mean he didn't have people that cared about him. And it doesn't mean that us caring has no meaning. That's one of your best qualities, Jo. Caring when no one else does. You see people—the real them. And that's something special."

"I thought I saw the real Blake," I said, stirring my cereal. "It turns out that I didn't. He was a drug addict and an armed robber. The only thing that probably had any meaning in his life was that yellow and black car he talked so much about. It was the only thing he looked excited about."

Dottie placed her hands on mine, her gaze intense. "Do you know where that car is now?"

I narrowed my eyes in suspicion. "No. The moment I mentioned it to the sheriff, he probably ran up to the community center and drove it to some super-secret hiding spot, where they searched it for evidence."

"Nothing is super-secret in Starlight Ridge," Dottie said, pushing herself back from the table. "So, let's go find that car."

I didn't move. "Why? Sheriff Hart probably already took all the good stuff."

"He might not have known what he was looking for," Dottie said, taking her bowl to the sink. "If there was anything illegal in the car like drugs or weapons, he's already seized those. But there is a lot you can learn about a person from something as simple as fast food bags and empty energy drink cans—more than you realize."

I watched my sister as she retrieved her coat from the closet. "What you're suggesting—it's not strictly legal, right? Going through the car of a murder victim amid an active investigation?"

I normally wouldn't question my sister on the legality of an action, especially if it could help us bring a murderer to justice. But this wasn't like Dottie, and it worried me. She should be the one hesitant to dig through a dead man's car. Not me.

Dottie turned to face me as she slid her arms into her coat.

"No, it's not legal. But we're not going to take anything. We're just looking."

I didn't move to stand. "Why are you doing this?"

Dottie released a hard breath and studied me, as if trying to decide how much to say. "You deciding that what you do doesn't matter and that it's not worth caring anymore—I'm not okay with that," she finally said. "And if this is what it takes to get my Jo back, then we're going to find this yellow and black car and see what it can tell us about Blake Sommer."

"You're doubtful it will help with the case," I said, pushing my chair back. It was a statement, not a question.

She nodded. "I am. Like you said, Sheriff Hart has already searched through the car."

"But you want to do it anyway. For me."

She leaned against the wall. "Yes. Maybe Blake didn't feel he had anyone in his life who cared, but you do. And that means something."

I looked at my uneaten cereal, then stood. I wasn't hungry anyway.

"Okay. Then let's check out this car. At the very least, I want to see if it really was as awesome as Blake claimed it was."

"There's just one thing," Dottie said. "We don't have the car keys."

"It's okay," I said, standing. "I'm pretty sure I know where the sheriff keeps them."

10

"Good morning, Sheriff," I said as I pushed open his office door, Dottie by my side. She was meant to be the distraction and she looked nervous, glancing behind her, like there might still be time to escape.

The sheriff, however, was not there. No one was.

This made things a lot easier, although Sheriff Hart really should have considered locking the doors while he was out. Any old person could walk in and help themselves to evidence. Or the half-eaten breakfast burrito still on the sheriff's desk. He must have left in a hurry.

I walked to the drawer where I'd seen the bullet casing and pulled on it.

It didn't budge.

It seemed the only reason it had been unlocked the previous evening was because the sheriff had been using it. It made me happy that he had enough common sense to lock up evidence—I had been worried he'd become too lax. Good for him. Bad for me.

"Dottie," I said, glancing over my shoulder. "You think you can pick a locked drawer?"

Dottie's lips opened, but no sound came out, and she glanced at the front door.

She was okay with me swiping the car keys, but the thought of doing it herself, and picking a lock, no less—that was beyond what she was comfortable with.

"It's okay," I said. "You don't need to do it."

This was one of those cases where it really was the thought that counted, and I was so grateful to Dottie for even coming here with me.

I turned to leave, but Dottie stopped me. "Wait." And then she pulled something out of her purse. A lock-picking kit. I hadn't realized she still had that old thing, let alone carried it around with her.

"Really, Dottie, I don't want you to feel like you have to do this—"

"Too late." And then Dottie walked over to the evidence drawer and laid out her tools. "You stay at the door and be the lookout," she said over her shoulder.

This wasn't an impromptu decision where Dottie felt coerced—she had known this might be the situation and she had come prepared.

"I didn't know you still had your set," I said, walking to the front door and taking my place.

She nodded as she worked on the lock. "I practice at

home sometimes. It's a form of meditation for me, and it keeps my mind strong."

And then she had the drawer open, just like that.

"You're fast," I said, impressed.

She looked back at me and smiled, her expression bright. It was a glimpse of the old Dottie, and I loved it. Illegal activity suited her.

"It helps that it's a cheap lock. Even you could have gotten it open without too much trouble."

I frowned. "Thanks for that compliment—I think."

She laughed. "It is one. Not many people can pick even a simple lock."

I walked over to the drawer and looked inside. Even with the drawer being full of odds and ends, I immediately spotted the evidence bag with the bullet casing, and next to it was a key fob. It had the VW symbol on them, and I was fairly certain that Blake had told me his car was a Volkswagen. I'd always loved a good German car.

I grabbed the key and moved to shut the drawer, but Dottie stopped me.

"What else did you take?" she asked, resting a hand on my sleeve.

Right.

I slipped my hand into my pocket and felt the lighter that had made its way in there.

"I swear I didn't take it on purpose," I started, but Dottie waved a hand in the air, stopping me.

She held a hand out to me. "Yes, I know. Just give it

back, please, before the sheriff realizes we've been rifling through his desk drawer."

I moved to place it in her hand but paused. "Think this was picked up from the explosion site?" I asked. "It was on top of everything else, right next to the evidence bag and Blake's car keys."

"I doubt it," Dottie said, trying to take the lighter from me. "If it had been from the explosion site, it would be in an evidence bag."

I moved the lighter out of her reach and held it up to the light. "There are scratches on it. Looks like initials."

"Lots of lighters have initials." Dottie glanced toward the front door, looking antsy. "Jo, we have to go. Please, just give it to me."

I held it out for her to see. "What does this look like? An E followed by an A?"

"Sure. Maybe." Dottie snatched the lighter from me just as the front door started to open.

I spun toward the door.

"You were supposed to be lookout," Dottie whispered.

"But your job was more interesting," I retorted, before half-running toward the door. It was my job to be a distraction, and a distraction I would be.

Sheriff Hart's deputy, Randy, was just stepping through the doorway when I reached him. The run had left me out of breath, and I leaned over, gasping for breath, blocking his entrance. "Randy, it's so good to see you. Beautiful day, isn't it?"

The deputy stared, seeming at a loss for words. "Jo, what are you doing here?" He tried stepping past me so he could shut the door, but I rested a hand on his shoulder, using him for support.

"I needed to talk to the sheriff, but after a thorough search of your office, he's nowhere to be found." I pulled in a long breath. "You'd think I'd be in better shape by now, but Dottie and I missed two weeks of parkour, and look what's happened. I told Dottie I was feeling more tired than usual and we couldn't skip parkour anymore, but she thought I was making it up. I'd say this proves otherwise."

"Why don't you have a seat so you can catch your breath and tell me what it is you need," Randy said, and he led me inside, pausing only to shut the front door. He turned to help me to a nearby chair but paused when he saw Dottie sitting at the sheriff's desk, scribbling a note of some sort.

It was a good thing he hadn't turned around any earlier because he would have seen her slipping her lock-picking set into her purse.

"Dottie, I'm sorry, I didn't see you," he said, looking startled.

Dottie smiled. "It's all right, Deputy. I'm just writing a quick note for the sheriff. I've been having trouble sleeping at night, wondering if this person who set off the explosion yesterday might do it again. The poor boy that died—he had no connections to Starlight Ridge, or the movie production team, which means it was a random attack and any one of us could be a target."

Wow, I always forgot how good a liar Dottie was when she wanted to be. It troubled me because she valued honesty above all else, and I didn't like that she felt she needed to lie right now.

"That's an awful feeling," Randy said, his expression a mixture of sympathy and concern. Guilt bubbled up in my stomach, and it made me want to come clean about every-thing. Deputy Randy was one of my favorite people in the world, and I hated that we were deceiving him.

"Randy, we know more than we're—" I started to say, and Dottie looked horrified at what I was about to do. Randy, however, cut me off before I could finish.

"I want to assure you both that Blake Sommer did have a connection here, and he appears to have been targeted. I don't believe you two, or anyone else, is in danger."

That shut me up.

Dottie and I exchanged shocked expressions. Maybe the sheriff had taken Frederick Alberheist seriously the previous evening, and maybe the sheriff was out arresting Eli Hunt right now.

"Does this mean that the movie is canceled?" I asked, unable to help the disappointment I felt. Yes, Eli Hunt was likely a murderer, but I doubted I'd ever have the chance to be in a Hollywood movie again. Maybe Sheriff Hart could wait until they were done filming to arrest the actor.

Both Randy and Dottie looked at me like they thought I was insane.

"That's what you're worried about right now?" Dottie asked at the same time that Randy asked, "Why would it be canceled?"

I chose to ignore Dottie's question because I didn't feel like being judged at the moment.

"Because you're arresting Eli Hunt. The movie isn't any good without its star."

Randy tilted his head to the side, his eyes scrutinizing. "Why would you think we're arresting Eli Hunt?"

"You said that Blake Sommer did have a connection here and he was targeted. Didn't the sheriff tell you that Eli Hunt and Blake had a history together? It didn't end well, and we think Blake came here to confront Eli."

Randy let a small smile escape. "Both of you thought that, or just you, Jo?"

Now that I thought back to it, I couldn't remember. "That's beside the point, because if it wasn't Eli Hunt who was targeting Blake..."

Oh, that sly devil. Frederick had been lying, just like we'd thought he might be. Then why had I chosen to believe him?

My gaze snapped up. "I dropped something on the beach the other day, and I think someone must have picked it up because when I returned, it was gone. Do you have a lost and found here that I can check?"

"What did you lose?" Randy asked slowly, as if he didn't trust me.

Good. I was happy to see that Sheriff Hart had been a positive influence and that the deputy had learned to be careful around me too.

"I lost...my lighter."

I knew it was risky, but I couldn't remember anything else that had been in that drawer. I'd panicked and said the first thing that came to mind—the only thing in that drawer that mattered to me.

"Your lighter," Randy said, looking dubious. "You don't smoke."

"No, but it has loads of other uses. Lighting candles on a cake, melting the ends of acrylic yarn when I'm done with a crochet project...starting a campfire."

"I didn't realize you enjoy camping," Randy said, looking amused.

His eyes were laughing at me, and I thought it rude that he didn't think I was capable of lighting a few twigs on fire.

"I don't, but I could if I wanted to. The point is, my lighter is very useful, and I'd like it back."

"All right," he said. "Let's see if we can find your lighter."

Maybe he hadn't learned to be as discerning when it came to me and my antics as I'd hoped.

Randy walked over to the sheriff's desk and tried the

drawer. I held my breath, praying that Dottie had had enough time to re-lock it.

The drawer didn't move.

I released my breath as the deputy took out his key and unlocked it.

"What color was your lighter?" he asked.

Oh. Color. Why couldn't I think of it? Then I thought of how the lights had reflected off its surface as I was trying to make out the initials on the side.

"Silver."

"You're in luck," he said, picking up the lighter and holding it up for me to see. "We picked this one up off the beach yesterday afternoon."

"Oh, thank goodness," I said, holding my hand out to take it from him. "I know I could get another lighter, but it's hard to find a good one that works with my wobbly fingers."

Dottie narrowed her eyes as Randy handed me the lighter. I was sure she didn't like the fact that she'd returned it to the drawer, only to have Randy give it back to me.

"Where did you find it?" I asked. "I looked everywhere for this thing."

I turned the lighter over, noticing how worn it appeared, the entire thing covered in scratches. The initials on the back that Dottie and I had noticed earlier could have easily been overlooked.

"Not far from the director's trailer, actually," Randy

said. "Or what's left of it. You're lucky it didn't get caught in the blast."

Yes. Lucky.

And it made me wonder. If Blake had been shot, had this lighter been used to cover it up? Maybe the explosion had just been a distraction.

Randy had said that Blake had been targeted, which meant that the sheriff had to know who had been doing the targeting.

Right?

Otherwise, how would Randy know that Dottie and I had no need to be worried?

Unless he'd only been saying it to placate us.

My attention returned to the lighter.

E.A.

I held the lighter under the sheriff's lamp so I could see it better. These darn eyes. I hated getting old.

My breath hitched. The bottom line of the E was actually a scratch. So, F.A.

I only knew one person who had those initials, and he did seem like the type of person who would be capable of blowing something up.

But if the sheriff believed that Frederick and not Eli, like I had assumed, had been targeting Blake, this lighter was evidence that he had missed something important.

11

"How do you know Blake was targeted?" I asked Randy.

"You know I can't tell you that, Jo." He glanced at the front door anxiously, likely expecting Sheriff Hart to burst through it at any second and accuse him of sharing information he shouldn't.

"This lighter," I said, holding it up. "You found it near the explosion site. And it has the initials F.A. on it. Does that mean anything to you?"

Randy tilted his head to the side. "I thought that was your lighter."

"I lied." Before he could act all disappointed in me, I added, "Really, Randy, you should have known. I've taught you better than that."

Randy stared for a brief second, probably wondering how I'd even known there was a lighter in the drawer to begin with, before giving me a slight smile and shaking his head. "You're putting me in a bad position here, Jo."

I held up the lighter again. "Why wasn't it in an evidence bag?"

Randy gave a weak shrug. "The explosion sent debris flying everywhere. It was difficult to know what came from the trailer and what had already been on the beach—people lose stuff out there all the time. Anything with burn or scorch marks was assumed to have come from the explosion, and anything else was considered lost and found."

"Of course the lighter wouldn't have scorch marks," Dottie said. "This isn't just any lighter, it's a pricy one. The good kind. And if it was used to set off the explosion, it wouldn't have been close enough to the flames anyhow. The arsonist either lost it, or they tossed it, trying to get rid of the evidence."

"I'm going to ask you again," I said, my voice firm but soft. "Do these initials mean anything to you?"

Randy hesitated, his gaze once again moving to the front door. "I'm not going to answer that. This is an active investigation, and the sheriff has been very clear that you are not a part of it."

I knew I had thought I wanted Randy to learn to be a good deputy and not give in so easily to people like me, but I wasn't liking it so much right now.

"It's okay, Jo. It doesn't mean anything, anyhow," Dottie said, placing a hand on my sleeve. She must have seen the frustration in my eyes. "Frederick might have visited Christopher to talk about the screenplay or complain about Leanne. Just because the sheriff found his lighter close by doesn't mean he was the one who killed Blake."

Randy's eyebrows popped up when Dottie mentioned Frederick, but he quickly masked his surprise.

I was unsure whether he was surprised that Dottie knew that Frederick was a suspect or if the thought of Frederick as a suspect had never crossed his mind.

I moved to hand the lighter back to Randy but then paused.

"What?" he asked, his hand extended, ready to take it back from me.

I put the lighter in my pocket. "Would you mind if I gave the lighter back to Frederick personally? I'm sure he's missing it. When we saw him last night, he had a cheap one that he couldn't do a thing with."

Randy seemed conflicted—he must have known I was up to something—but he couldn't think of a reason why not, so he nodded. "All right. Like I said, it's not evidence, and that's one less thing in our lost and found."

"Thank you, dear," I said, patting my pocket. "It means a lot." I turned to Dottie. "Shall we go?"

Now Dottie seemed conflicted. The item in my pocket was much more than a lighter, and it seemed to weigh heavily on her conscience.

"Of course," she said, forcing a smile.

We waved goodbye to the deputy, then pushed through the front door and out into the sun.

Per her usual, Dottie tilted her head up, soaking up the warmth. The constant sun was Dottie's favorite part of living in Starlight Ridge, especially on cool days like today.

"What should our first stop be?" I asked as we walked away from the sheriff's office. "I have no idea where Frederick is or if he's even still in town, so should we find the car first?"

Dottie didn't say anything, instead stopping to fix her shoe. I saw the subtle glance behind her. The way she walked after she straightened. She was in cop mode.

"What's going on?" I whispered.

Dottie smiled brightly and laughed like I had just said something hilarious. "We're being followed," she said through her smile.

I tried to not look alarmed as I grinned. "Who is it?" I didn't dare look behind us to see who. Dottie would never let me hear the end of it if we spooked our stalker. "It's Frederick, isn't it."

Dottie shook her head. "No, it's Deputy Randy. He's smarter than we give him credit for. I don't think he knows about the car keys, but he suspects something about you and that lighter."

"That might not be a bad thing," I said, my lips pulling into a frown. "If Frederick is the one who set off the explosion, I wouldn't mind having law enforcement tailing us when we go talk to him."

"True, but we can't go find Blake's car as long as the deputy is following us, and as grumpy as Frederick is, I doubt he would do anything to a couple of old women."

"You never know. I've thought that about all the murderers who have tried to hurt us." I paused. "Think Frederick is still in town? He could have left after the vigil last night. Leanne made it clear that he wasn't wanted here."

Dottie paused to catch her breath. "Frederick doesn't seem like the kind of guy who scares easily. My guess is that he visited Christopher before Leanne confronted him. If you want to get things done, you go to the person in charge—the one who can actually make decisions. Leanne doesn't want Frederick on set or messing with her screenplay, but that doesn't mean she has the power to stop him."

"So, you think that Christopher told Frederick to leave town. If things didn't end well between the director and Frederick, that could be motive to blow up the trailer. And a warning to anyone else who tried to stand in his way." I offered Dottie my arm. She linked her hand through it, and then we continued up the road. "He still following us?"

She nodded. "Yup."

We rounded a corner. Down the boardwalk, I could see the film crew preparing to shoot a scene in front of Adeline's chocolate shop. Even though we were outside, lights were being strategically placed around the shop and large trucks rumbled by, parking across the boardwalk.

"Let's say that Frederick did blow up Christopher's trailer," Dottie said. "That doesn't explain why he shot Blake."

She made a good point.

"What if the two aren't connected?" I asked, steering Dottie toward the scuba shop. I would have preferred visiting the chocolate shop, but there was no way we were getting through there while they were filming, and we needed somewhere to wait until the deputy got tired of following us. "What if someone else shot Blake inside Christopher's trailer, and then Frederick blew it up, not realizing someone was inside?"

Dottie's eyes lit up, as they had more often recently when we'd been talking about the investigation. She claimed she hated getting involved, and that was true, but I also knew she missed being in the field. As much as she respected Sheriff Hart and Deputy Randy, she enjoyed being a part of things again.

"You're saying it wasn't a coverup—it was a happy accident," Dottie said. "For the shooter, of course. Not Blake. And certainly not Frederick."

If we were looking at two separate incidents, though, that made things infinitely more complicated.

"If Frederick is the arsonist," I said, my words slow, "does that make Eli Hunt the shooter? Maybe he and Blake really did have a checkered past."

I hated the thought of it. Even though I'd only met the actor briefly, I'd liked him.

"It seems unwise to follow that path of logic," Dottie said, following me into the scuba shop. "I don't trust that screenwriter—he was out to make trouble."

"Just because he was out to make trouble doesn't mean it wasn't true. A hurtful truth is far more damaging than a hurtful lie because it can be proven true."

I glanced back through the display window, looking for Deputy Randy. I couldn't see him—he must have been waiting to the side of the shop. We'd lie low here for a few minutes until he found something better to do.

"Are you confident in your ability to discern truth from lies?" Dottie asked, turning toward me. "You'd bet someone's guilt or innocence on it?"

I felt I was quite good at reading people—it was how I had been able to help the sheriff like I had over the past couple of years—but would I bet someone else's life on it?

"No, I suppose I wouldn't," I said.

"Dottie and Jo," Caleb said, walking in from the back of the store. We'd obviously caught him by surprise. "You two finally decide you want to take me up on my offer of scuba lessons?"

Dottie snorted. "Thanks, but no thanks. I'd be akin to a sunken ship."

Caleb laughed, but whatever he was going to say next was cut off by his toddler sprinting around him and into the shop.

"Sorry," his wife Bree said, running after the boy. "I told him it's bath time, and well, you can see how that went."

"No bath," the boy yelled, before giggling and crawling under a rack of swimsuits.

Bree gave us a tired smile before saying, "Oh, that's too bad, because whoever takes a bath right now gets a cookie when they are done. It looks like no one here wants a cookie."

The boy's head popped out from behind the rack. "I want a cookie." And then he raced past us and into the back of the store.

"I'm not above bribery," she said, before disappearing after her son.

"No one is," I called after her.

Dottie looked offended. "I am."

I laughed. "Maybe as a cop, but what about last week when I offered you a couple days off from work in exchange for you cleaning out the kitty litter for the week? You snapped that up pretty quick."

"I don't know why you hate cleaning out Skittles' box so much," Dottie said with a frown. "And that wasn't bribery, it was an exchange."

"That's all that bribery is," I said. "Caleb and Bree's son received a cookie in exchange for taking a bath."

"Jo has a point," Caleb said. We heard a screech from upstairs, and Caleb glanced toward the back of the store. "I better go check on that. It seems that bribery might not have been enough in this case." And then he sprinted away.

Dottie didn't look happy that Caleb had agreed with me.

I smiled, however, quite pleased with myself. But as I thought on Caleb's words, it faded.

"What?" Dottie asked, her brows dipping in concern.

"No one is above bribery," I said, my words slow.

"And?"

"Frederick wanted nothing more than to be involved in this screenplay," I said, as if I knew what I was talking about. "He had been Leanne's mentor, frustrated with the quality of screenplays that were being produced in Hollywood, and he intended for her to take his place when he retired. But then Eli Hunt chose her screenplay as his debut as a producer. She was receiving recognition and praise, and Frederick was jealous of the very thing he had created. He wanted credit for his part in helping mold Leanne it was him who had been responsible for connecting her with Eli Hunt in the first place, after all. But no one was recognizing it. Not Christopher, and not Eli."

"I'm sure the sheriff knows all of this already," Dottie said. "And it has nothing to do with either Christopher or Blake Sommer. Why kill a childhood rival of Eli's or blow up the trailer of the one person who can help you?"

"It does seem farfetched," I conceded. "But then why does Frederick know so much about Eli Hunt's past? No one in the world had heard of Blake Sommer until yesterday, but Frederick had. If he is to be believed, he knew quite a bit about Blake. It doesn't make sense."

"You think Frederick dug into Eli's background to come up with something he could blackmail Eli with," Dottie guessed. "Something that would put Frederick back into the limelight."

I held up a finger as my mind worked through everything. "What if Frederick discovered who Blake was? We don't actually know who Blake was, but we know that he likely gave false information when he was checking in as a background actor. The guy didn't even know his own phone number. That tells me that he wasn't here for reconciliation with Eli. He was here for revenge. He wanted to destroy Eli and do it without anyone knowing he'd been here."

Dottie looked perplexed. "You think Frederick and Blake were working together? What could Blake possibly do for Frederick that he couldn't do himself?"

"Blow up a trailer, giving Frederick an alibi," I said, feeling pleased with myself. "And if Blake was already intent on destroying Eli Hunt's movie, it wouldn't have been difficult to convince him to go along with it. It could be that Frederick offered to pay Blake to do something he'd intended to do all along."

Dottie was quiet for a moment. "That doesn't explain who shot Blake."

Oh, right. If Frederick killed Blake to cover his tracks, he'd have had to do it at the same time as the explosion.

That also meant that Frederick wouldn't have had the alibi he needed. In that case, Frederick might as well have just set off the explosion himself.

"Unless Frederick wasn't the one to shoot Blake," I said.

"Now we have a third person?" Dottie asked. She shook her head. "This is all getting too complicated. I'm sorry, but wild conjectures won't get us anywhere."

Dottie was right, and I didn't have much more than that. I never did. I got through life on conjecture, and it had always worked out for me in the past.

"We can verify a lot of it by talking with Eli," I said. "All we need to do is catch him off guard, maybe when he's distracted on set. He seems the type to accidentally spill secrets to a couple old ladies."

Dottie sighed and shook her head, wanting me to know how much she didn't like the new plan. But I also knew she had resigned herself to follow it. Because she loved me. And because she enjoyed having a mystery to solve, even if she wouldn't admit it.

"I liked it better when our plan was to look through a pretty car," she said.

"I did too, but here we are." I peered through the front window. "Think Deputy Randy is still out there?"

"It's been long enough, I think he's probably gotten bored."

I pushed open the door and stuck my head out, looking up and down the boardwalk. The deputy was nowhere in sight. Looked like my sister was right. I motioned for her to follow me and then walked back out onto the street.

The door of the scuba shop hadn't even had time to close behind us when a shot rang out.

A gunshot.

Dottie threw herself onto me, pushing me to the ground and covering my head.

Both of my knees and my right elbow slammed into the concrete, and I instantly found myself wishing my sister didn't love me so much.

12

It had only been one gunshot. But it had been one too many.

My heart raced and my ears rang.

"You couldn't have been a little gentler?" I asked Dottie. I was going to have at least a few bruises from the landing.

"I was saving your life," Dottie said, rolling to her side and then pushing herself into a sitting position. She seemed surprised that I wasn't more grateful.

I was grateful. We didn't know where the shot had come from, and she'd placed my life above hers.

But that didn't mean it hadn't hurt.

"I know, and I love you for it," I told her, grabbing onto a pipe sticking out from the scuba shop's wall and pulling myself onto my feet. I then helped Dottie up the rest of the way. Without missing a beat, she turned and pointed toward Adeline's chocolate shop. Right now, she was all business.

"The shot came from down there."

With all the people still running around the movie set, I couldn't see a thing.

"It was Frederick who fired the shot," I said. "It had to be."

Dottie glanced at me. "No, it didn't have to be."

"Christopher's trailer wasn't a scare tactic—it was meant to take out the director. It didn't, though, and now Frederick just finished the job. Or he tried to."

Dottie shook her head with a patient smile. "We don't know who was shot, if anyone. The gun could have been a prop for the movie."

If it had been a prop for the movie, why was there so much chaos, and why was Deputy Randy herding people away from the shop? He had just started putting up the police tape when he spotted Dottie and me.

"Oh, no you don't," the deputy said, ducking under the tape and blocking our path. "This is a crime scene. I just got off the phone with the sheriff, and he has made it clear that you two aren't invited."

"Fine. We're not invited," I said, placing my hands on my hips. "But we at least have a right to know who was shot. We have friends in this town, you know. And one of them happens to own this chocolate shop."

Deputy Randy's hesitated, but then he glanced back to see the sheriff hurrying toward him.

He gave us a helpless shrug. "Sorry, this is an active crime scene." And then he walked away, likely afraid that if he stayed any longer, we'd get him tell us everything.

He wasn't wrong.

"Frederick shot Christopher. It's the only thing that makes sense," I mumbled.

All film crew were escorted away from the shop, and the sheriff began speaking with each of them individually. As they waited for their turn, they looked anxious, like they were about to be the one accused of shooting someone.

Dottie turned away from the chocolate shop. "The only reason you think Frederick Alberheist blew up that trailer is because you found a lighter," she said. "It proves that at some point since Frederick arrived in Starlight Ridge, he was on the beach. Just like everyone else here in town. Yes, he is a bit on the grumpy side and does seem to have some very strong opinions, but that doesn't make him a murderer. It was harsh of you to jump to that conclusion."

"It's not like you were stopping me."

Dottie glanced back at me, her brows furrowed in annoyance. "The only thing I agreed to was looking through Blake's car." And she now looked like she was regretting it.

"Well, who do you think is our murderer?" I asked, crossing my arms.

I knew I was being childish, and the way Dottie was looking at me, she thought so too. But two people had been shot in the past two days, and a trailer had been rigged to explode.

There was a murderer in our town, and someone needed to stop them.

"You're scared," Dottie said, her expression softening. "I understand that. But that's when people start getting sloppy. Even law enforcement. I'm not saying Frederick isn't a suspect, but he can't be the only suspect."

My gaze dropped. It wasn't Dottie's fault that she was right.

"I know," I mumbled. "We still have to consider Eli Hunt and..."

Was there anyone else?

"Christopher is still a viable suspect," Dottie said.

"But it was his trailer that blew up."

She nodded. "He knows that trailer better than anyone, and if he was trying to cover something up, I'm sure he'd know exactly how to do it."

I glanced back toward the chocolate shop. Movement caught my eye. Jennifer, the production assistant. She was with her two friends, and they were hurrying across the beach. The way they kept glancing over their shoulders, it seemed they were trying to slip away unnoticed.

But why?

"Hold that thought," I told Dottie, starting toward the beach. "I need some fresh air."

Dottie's eyebrows furrowed in confusion. "But we're already—" She followed my gaze. "Of course. The last time you needed fresh air was when we were already outside and you wanted to talk to those three. Seems to have become a pattern with you."

"They're up to something." My steps quickened.

"It doesn't matter," Dottie protested as she struggled to catch up. "They don't trust you any more than they did the last time you tried. You didn't learn anything useful then, so what makes you think they'll talk to you now?"

I slowed my steps and waited for Dottie. "Because a second person has been shot, and they're scared."

"Scared people clam up," Dottie said.

It looked like Jennifer and her friends were heading for the large rock outcrop. Over time, the rock had eroded and a cave had formed. There was plenty of space inside, and no one would know you were there until they were practically on top of you. The perfect hiding spot.

"And some people panic when they are scared and can't stop talking," I told her. "I'm counting on the blond guy for that."

As we drew closer to the outcrop, I held a finger up to my lips.

For three people who were trying to hide, they weren't very quiet. They were arguing, quite loudly, cigarette smoke wafting through the air.

"They're going to think it was us," one of the men said. It sounded like the blond.

"Why? You have zero motive, Zack," Jennifer said.

The other man spoke up. "We're the only ones who

aren't supposed to be here, Jen. You don't think they'll find that suspicious?"

A pause.

"I'll tell them you're my brothers. You had never been on a movie set before and you begged me to let you come along."

"People bring their family members on set all the time, and yet you lied to get us on this one. What will they make of that?"

Another pause. "Do you have a better idea, Tank? They can't prove anything."

A sneeze.

Unfortunately, the sneeze hadn't come from Jennifer or her friends.

It had come from Dottie.

I whipped toward her, and her eyes widened. "Sorry," she whispered.

I immediately dropped to the sand and began rubbing my knee, as if I'd injured it. I made a point of never being on the ground if I could help it, because I could rarely get back up, and the beach sand would make it next to impossible.

But desperate times called for desperate measures, and we had a bigger problem at the moment—Jennifer and her two friends, who were now standing over me, their eyes narrowed.

"How long have you been listening?" the sharp-nosed man asked.

I blinked at him, giving him the most innocent expression I could muster. "Tank, so good to see you again." His lips parted in surprise at me using his name, but I pretended not to notice. "We've only been here long enough for me to trip and twist my knee. Dr. Patty says I shouldn't be walking on the sand without some sort of support, and it looks like she was right." I held a hand up. "Would you?"

Tank looked back at the others, the silent question in his eyes of what he was supposed to do in a situation like this.

"I haven't got all day," I said impatiently. I waved my hand at him. "Blake Sommer was a gentleman and helped me up when I was stuck in a metal chair. I'm sure you can manage just as well as he did."

Tank took my hand, though I knew it was the last thing he wanted to do, then gave me his other arm to hold onto. I had been right. Getting up out of the sand turned out to be quite the workout for both Tank and me, but we managed it, and I dusted the sand off my clothes.

Tank, now breathing heavily, turned back to the other two. "What are we supposed to do about them?"

Oh, dear. That wasn't a promising way to start our conversation.

"You don't need to do anything about us," I said, pretending to misunderstand. "I can walk myself over to Dr. Patty's clinic. Don't you worry about a thing."

Tank looked like he was holding back an eye roll.

That was good. He thought I really was clueless.

"I'm not worried," Tank said. "About your knee, at least."

Dottie folded her arms across her chest. "No, you're worried because we know you're not supposed to be here."

Her statement didn't just shock Jennifer and her two friends—I nearly fell over from surprise.

I gave her a look that was supposed to mean *What do you think you're doing?*, but Dottie wouldn't even look at me.

"So, what's your deal?" she asked them. "You guys show up in our quiet little town—people start dying, trailers start exploding. I'm guessing drugs. Did Blake steal some from you?"

Zack, the blond, shook his head vigorously, looking shocked at the allegation. "Oh, no. I would never do drugs. I had a cousin that did all that, and now he's dead."

He was more concerned about me thinking he was a drug user than about accidentally giving us information, and his friends didn't seem to think much of that.

"Zack," Jennifer whispered—it held a warning.

The message was received, and Zack immediately pressed his lips together.

"Okay, no drugs," Dottie said, her words slow as she thought through the most likely scenarios. She turned to Jennifer. "I don't think it's Blake Sommer you had a problem with—it's Christopher. Maybe you've worked with him before and it didn't go so well. You made sure you were hired to work on this film so you could have a bit of revenge, and these guys came along to help make sure it went smoothly." She paused. "Of course, if that was the goal, I don't think they've earned their paychecks."

It was Jennifer's turn to balk. "You think I have a problem with Christopher?" She laughed. "I have nothing but respect for the man—everyone does. There isn't a person here who would wish ill on the man."

Dottie tilted her head to the side. "But his trailer blew up. And someone just shot him on his own movie set."

My sister had no way of knowing who had been shot, and I knew she wouldn't just throw out baseless accusations. She was getting Jennifer to talk without her even knowing it.

Damn, Dottie was good.

Jennifer stopped laughing, her eyebrows scrunched in confusion. "It wasn't Christopher who was shot." She looked between Dottie and me. "It was Frederick Alberheist. He's dead."

13

I stared. "That can't be right."

    I wasn't used to being wrong—he was my prime suspect.

"He should have left town when he had the chance," Dottie murmured, shaking her head. When she saw the curious looks that Jennifer and her friends were giving her, she clarified, "We heard Leanne Warner tell him he wasn't allowed to be on set anymore."

Jennifer raised a shoulder. "I don't know what to tell you, because he's been on set every day." She paused. "No one was happy about it, of course, but there was nothing we could do about it."

"Why didn't Christopher just kick him out?" Dottie asked, her words slow, like she was thinking aloud.

"Because Christopher was scared of him," Jennifer said matter-of-factly.

I studied her for a moment, quiet. She glanced at me, looking uneasy.

"What?" she finally asked.

I let her squirm for another moment before answering. "You're Christopher's right-hand woman, right? You are the production assistant, and you know everything that goes on around there. You help calm the storms and keep things running smoothly, or as smoothly as they can on a movie set. And yet, when a man was murdered, you ran away. That's not a good look for you. If you ask me, I don't think Christopher was the only one who was scared."

Jennifer hesitated and looked between Tank and Zack.

"Oh, leave Jennifer be," Dottie said. "Two people have died, and I'm sure she's terrified that the sheriff's sights are going to settle on her. Like you said, she's everywhere on that set, making sure things run smoothly, and they obviously haven't. The last thing she needs is you making things harder."

How unlike Dottie to side with someone who was obviously acting suspiciously.

I hadn't realized what she was doing until I saw that Jennifer's complexion had gone pale.

"Why would the sheriff think I had anything to do with Frederick's death?" she asked, her gaze panicked. "I've never even spoken to Frederick. I was told I couldn't even make direct eye contact."

Dottie shrugged. "Maybe because of the company you

keep." She nodded to Tank and Zack. "You haven't exactly been playing by the rules."

Tank's tough exterior dissolved, and his expression became as panicked as Jennifer's. "But we didn't cause any trouble—not the kind the sheriff would be interested in. Were we disappointed when Christopher turned us down? Of course. Did we push a little when we should have backed off? Yes. But we took his last warning to heart and are set to leave Starlight Ridge first thing tomorrow morning."

"You're leaving town immediately after the second death in as many days," Dottie said, tsking. "Sheriff Hart isn't going to appreciate that."

Did Dottie actually know what Tank was talking about or was she acting like she did? Because I, for one, had no idea what was going on right now.

Zack started pacing, running a hand through his hair. "Approach Christopher directly, you said. We'll only end up in a slush pile if we don't. It's worth the risk." He spun to face Tank. "You said that this is how all screenwriters do it. That if we didn't come out here, no one would pay any attention to us—that we'd never have another opportunity like this."

Tank held up his hands in a defensive gesture, no longer recognizable as the tough man he'd portrayed himself to be. "This isn't my fault."

Zack was breathing heavily like he was having a panic attack. He stopped his pacing and looked directly at Tank.

"How's it going to look when Christopher tells the sheriff that two wannabes kept hounding him with their script, and that he turned them down multiple times? That he told us he already had plenty of projects on his plate and didn't have time to read what we'd traveled all this way to bring him? And then Christopher's trailer blows up and one of the most talented screenwriters ever is shot to death." He sank to the sand. "How is that going to look, Tank?"

Whatever was happening here, it was obvious that these two men had not killed Frederick Alberheist. Either that or they were very good actors. No offense to them, but I didn't think it was the latter.

"I was only trying to help," Jennifer said, her voice soft. "I'm sorry, I never should have agreed to get you on set. I thought Christopher would see how passionate you two are and give you a chance, but he was right—he's busy. He's got so much going on with this movie, and I should have known that this wasn't the way to do it." She shook her head. "It's all my fault."

Dottie's lips turned down into a frown as she looked between the friends. "Oh, stop it. You can pout all you want, but that's not going to help you out of this mess. What we need are answers. Which means that the three of you better start telling us all you know." When Jennifer and her two friends glanced at one another, no one talking, Dottie released an exasperated sigh. "Now would be nice. If you want to keep yourselves out of jail, that is."

That got them speaking. Unfortunately, it was all at once.

As they talked over each other, Dottie released an ear-splitting whistle. "Jennifer, we're starting with you. You know Christopher best, and you're on set every day. Is there someone that is tied to all three of our victims?"

"Three?" Jennifer asked with a blank look.

Dottie took a moment to pull in a deep breath, and then with a patient voice, she said, "Blake Sommer, Christopher, and Frederick."

"Christopher's not dead."

"No, but his trailer blew up, which means he's still a victim. That explosion could have been meant for him."

Jennifer nodded that she understood, then was quiet as she thought. "I don't think Blake was here in Starlight Ridge long enough to be connected to anyone," she finally said. "Christopher and Frederick were obviously connected, and it was Leanne Warner that had most of the interactions with both of them. Her and Eli Hunt. They all run in the same circles, but neither Leanne nor Eli could have done anything like this."

Dottie and I exchanged glances.

Eli Hunt. I liked the guy, I really did. But what Jennifer didn't know was that Eli Hunt was connected to all three of the victims, and we didn't have anything else to go on.

"Tell us more about Eli Hunt," I told Jennifer. "Anything that you've observed or heard from others."

Jennifer's eyebrows scrunched in confusion. "You're not

honestly saying you think it was him, are you? Because there's no way. Eli Hunt is your 'boy next door' kind of guy. He's sweet, if not a little eccentric. Treats everyone with respect, even the little guys, you know? That's rare to find in a successful actor like him."

"What do you mean by eccentric?" Dottie asked, homing in on that one word, as if she hadn't heard anything else that Jennifer had said.

Jennifer raised a shoulder. "You know he's a method actor, right? He behaves as if he's actually his character. Eli Hunt isn't from the UK, but he's been talking with a British accent since he got here. He dresses in leather jackets and has his hair slicked back like he's in the movie *Grease*. Once they wrap on the film, he'll go back to being Eli Hunt, until the next movie, where he might be a professor who moonlights as a boxer or something weird like that."

I smiled, hoping it conveyed that we were grateful for her help.

"I'm not sure that makes him a 'boy next door,'" Dottie said. "His character in this movie starts out pretty rough. Maybe Eli took this method acting thing of his too far."

Jennifer was already shaking her head. "No way. It couldn't have been him. I'd bet my life on it."

"What about theirs?" Dottie asked, pointing to Tank and Zack.

Their eyes widened.

If Dottie had been going for shock value, she'd achieved it.

"You don't think we're actually viable suspects, do you?" Tank asked. He looked like he didn't want to believe it but also like he was afraid of what our answer to that might be.

Zack just looked plain scared.

"Of course not," I said. "As long as you come clean to the sheriff and tell him everything you know, he has no reason to think you had anything to do with this. You didn't know anyone except Jennifer before coming here."

"Well…" Tank said, now looking uncomfortable.

"Right?" I prompted, nervous about what his answer was going to be.

"Before we came to deliver our script to Christopher in person, we might have sent a copy in the mail," Zack said. "Followed by a few letters. One of which was written when Tank was drunk and angry at being ghosted."

Dottie looked at Tank in horror. "Please tell me you didn't threaten Christopher."

Tank hesitated, and that was all it took.

"Nope. I'm out," Dottie said, throwing her arms into the air. "You are making this way too easy for the sheriff to pin these murders on you, and I won't be involved." She spun around and walked away as quickly as she was able, which wasn't very fast, considering she was a seventy-one-year-old trying to walk through sand.

I left a horrified-looking Tank and hurried after Dottie. "You know they didn't do it," I said, catching up to her. "And they need someone in their corner. Who do you think people are going to want to see go down for these murders—a beloved and well-respected actor who just so happens to be one of the biggest stars in the world or a couple of angry unsuccessful screenwriters?"

Dottie's steps slowed, and she leaned on her cane. "I hate when you make good points."

"Trust me, I do too," I said.

Dottie sighed and turned to me. "I don't care what's in those letters—they need to tell the sheriff everything they know before he discovers it on his own. It will be much better for them."

"I agree." My gaze landed on the boardwalk, where the crime scene tape was still up and the ambulance was just pulling away. I squinted my eyes.

"Who is that?" Dottie asked, looking in the same direction.

On the other side of the beach, a small figure was waving their arms in our direction, like they were trying to get our attention.

"It's Isaac," I said. "I'm sure he's cursing that wheelchair right now."

Isaac wasn't used to being constricted like this, unable to travel over the sand on his own, and Dottie and I were moving at a painfully slow pace.

As we drew closer, I saw that his expression was panicked, and the moment we stepped off the sand, Isaac said to Dottie, "You have to help her."

"Help who?" Dottie asked, her eyebrows raised.

Isaac continued, as if he hadn't heard her. "The sheriff won't listen to me, but he respects your opinion. You were a cop, and he knows you do things by the book. Please, talk to him and tell him she didn't do it."

Dottie's gaze subconsciously went to my pocket, where the keys to Blake's car were. I knew she was feeling an enormous amount of guilt right now, Isaac's words reminding her how she felt about going behind the sheriff's back. I hoped she didn't feel guilty enough to go give him back the keys before we'd had a chance to look at anything.

"What are you talking about, Isaac?" I asked him, my voice gentle. "Who is it that you want us to help?"

Isaac's gaze moved to me, and he seemed surprised that I was even there. Guess he saw Dottie as a one-woman show. I tried not to be offended.

"Leanne, of course." He looked between us. "You didn't hear? Not even ten minutes after arriving at the chocolate shop, Sheriff Hart sent his deputy to arrest my fiancée. He says she killed Frederick Alberheist."

14

Dottie and I burst into the sheriff's office—or at least we tried to. It was actually quite slow, as I was having trouble with the front door. It had been a long day, and I had to use all my body weight to push it open while Dottie walked in after me.

When we finally made it inside, our presence was no surprise. Sheriff Hart stood from his desk chair with a look that said, *You've got to be kidding me.*

"I take it you heard, along with the rest of the town, that I've arrested Leanne."

"But you know she didn't do it," I said, marching up to him. "You sit next to her in church every Sunday—that has to count for something."

The sheriff smirked. "How would you know? You haven't been for months."

The community center hosted bingo right after church,

and ever since they'd gotten rid of the 'Salvation' bingo card, an extra card given out for going to church, I hadn't attended services.

"You always sat on the same row as her and Isaac for the year when I did go," I said. "People have unofficial assigned seats, and you wouldn't go messing that up—not when the town is just starting to like you."

Sheriff Hart pretended his feelings had been hurt. "They didn't like me?"

It was my turn to smile. "You've arrested both me and Isaac in the past couple years, so yeah, they've been slow to trust. But they're warming up. Of course, that was before you arrested Leanne—I don't think that's going to go down very well with them."

"No, it's not," Leanne called from the single jail cell in the far corner of the room. I'd forgotten she could hear every word we were saying—I kind of liked that about our old-timey sheriff's office.

Sheriff Hart raised his gaze to the ceiling, like he didn't know what he was going to do with us.

Dottie cleared her throat. "I know you can't share anything about an active investigation," she started.

The sheriff's gaze settled on her. "But you want me to anyway." He seemed surprised that she'd even suggest it.

Dottie gave a curt nod, even as she shifted uncomfortably on her feet. "Mind if I have a seat? My feet are killing me."

Sheriff Hart gestured to a chair on the other side of his desk. "Please do."

Isaac had said Sheriff Hart respected Dottie's opinion, and I couldn't help the jealousy that bubbled up—the sheriff would never offer me a seat at his desk, especially if I was trying to get information about an active investigation. If I had come by myself, he'd probably have already thrown me out.

Dottie walked slowly to the seat and eased herself into it. Once she'd gotten comfortable, she turned her attention back to the sheriff. "I'm curious why you're arresting Leanne when you have more viable suspects."

"Thank you," Leanne called. "I've been asking him the same question. Maybe I'll finally get an answer to it."

The sheriff gave Dottie a weak smile as he sat down across from her. "Her husband was a lot quieter when he was back there. I miss the good ol' days."

Dottie raised an eyebrow. "The good old days when you made a habit of arresting innocent people? I don't think those days are in the past for you."

Sheriff Hart stiffened. "That's not fair. You of all people should know that you need to follow where the evidence leads. Even if you don't like it."

That shut Dottie up, and her gaze dropped.

"You know how much scrutiny I'm under in a town like this," the sheriff continued, his voice softening. "Nothing I do is ever right, so I have to ignore what people are saying about me and just do the job in the best way I know how. That doesn't make it easy."

Dottie's gaze lifted, and she gave a slight nod. "I know."

"Then you have to trust that I'm going over everything countless times—anything to make sure I get it right."

She gave another nod. "I do trust you."

I could see the guilt was eating her alive. She'd stepped over the line and joined me as a rogue investigator, and she was regretting it.

"I hope that's true," the sheriff said. And then he held out a hand.

Dottie stared at it, and my stomach sank.

"The keys," he said. "I know you have them."

Her gaze whipped to me, and it held accusation.

"You think I told him?" I asked. "You know me better than that."

Sheriff Hart pointed to a corner behind me. I turned, and there, at the top of a wall, was a camera. I swiveled my head and realized there were others placed strategically around the room.

"When did you get those?" I asked. Just a couple of years ago, this place had been vacant, except for the rats.

The sheriff looked like he was trying not to laugh at my surprise. "A few months ago. This town has murder rates per capita that would rival any big city. Those security cameras were long overdue."

"Starlight Ridge didn't used to be this way," I said. "It

started right about the same time you became sheriff. Not that I'm implying anything."

Sheriff Hart leaned back in his chair and folded his arms across his chest. "No, it all started with the death of your eldest sister, if I'm not mistaken. Since then, this town has had a murder a year, sometimes two. That's nothing for Chicago, but it means something in a little place like Starlight Ridge. Especially when it's more often the visitors who get the raw end of the deal."

I stilled. He was right, but I found it most offensive of him to mention our sister.

The sheriff immediately realized his mistake, and his expression fell. "I'm sorry. I didn't mean it like that. Of course it's not your fault, or your sister's. I only meant— well, I don't really know what I meant. I just..."

Sheriff Hart was struggling, and I was content to let him.

Dottie, however, took pity on him and held her hand out to me. She wanted the car key. There was no use fighting it, so I dug the key out of my pocket and placed it in her hand. "You're saying our family is bad luck," she said, placing the key on the sheriff's desk. "And maybe we are."

"That's not what I was saying," he said, and then in an attempt to change the subject, he asked, "Discover anything interesting in the car?"

Before Dottie could admit that we hadn't found the car,

let alone been inside it, I said, "You got most of the good stuff, but we didn't come away empty-handed."

Dottie glanced at me, an eyebrow raised. I met her gaze and refused to look away—I wouldn't be shamed into admitting we'd never found the car. My sister hated when I was dishonest, and it was true that I often felt the need to lie, especially in situations like this. It was an impulse I had spent my entire life battling. The problem was that the impulse had served me so well in the past couple of years, I struggled to understand why it was bad.

If it put bad guys behind bars, what was the harm?

Sheriff Hart studied me, likely also wondering if I was to be believed. "You didn't find anything," he finally said. "Deputy Randy and I went over that thing with a fine-tooth comb. Aside from some questionable dietary choices evidenced by the mounds of fast-food receipts, and an unhealthy obsession with Eli Hunt, the guy was clean."

I tried to stay calm and not show how big a deal that statement had been.

What had led the sheriff to believe Blake was obsessed with Eli Hunt, and why didn't he seem worried about it?

I was caught in a conundrum. If I asked the sheriff about it and he hadn't removed the evidence from the car, not thinking it was important, he'd know we'd never been inside. And as long as the sheriff believed we'd been inside the car, he would be more likely to share information with us.

"You're right," I said, acting guilty, like he'd caught me

in a lie. "We didn't find anything useful. It does lead me to wonder what it is about celebrities that makes people so crazy. Blake had told me he drove all the way down here, just so he could be in a movie with Eli Hunt."

"I believe it," Sheriff Hart said. "You saw the pictures of Eli that he'd printed off the internet and the list of all scheduled appearances that Eli Hunt was supposed to be at. Including the shoot dates for this movie."

"We sure this guy wasn't dangerous?" Dottie asked, frowning.

This was good. We were talking more like friends than investigators. Sheriff Hart had let his guard down.

Sheriff Hart chuckled and shook his head. "You've never lived in LA before, have you. There are all sorts of people whose sole identity is based on celebrity sightings —their walls are covered in pictures and autographs they've managed to capture. They're not dangerous, just... lonely."

I supposed I could understand that.

"So, you think Blake's death was accidental, then," I said. "An unfortunate case of being in the wrong place at the wrong time."

"You don't?" the sheriff asked, studying me closely.

We were back to being investigators, it seemed.

"No," I said. "Blake was supposed to be with me on that shuttle, waiting to drive onto set. Why would he rush outside and get in a car with someone else?"

Sheriff Hart's curiosity morphed into annoyance. "Are

you saying that someone picked up Blake just minutes before his death?"

Oh, dear. I could have sworn I'd told the sheriff about that.

"We've talked about you sharing information that could be pertinent to my cases," he said, exhaustion in his voice.

I raised a finger. "Actually, you said you didn't want me involved with your cases—"

"Which you obviously are, despite my threats," he interrupted. "I should arrest you and Dottie for stealing evidence and interfering with an active investigation."

"But you won't," I said. "Because you like us, and we're useful."

"You're not that useful. You don't even know who was driving," Sheriff Hart said. He was in one of his grumpy moods, and I suddenly wondered if he really would arrest us. My sister would not be happy with me if he did.

"I know who picked him up," Leanne called from the cell in the corner. I'd forgotten she was there.

"And who would that be?" Sheriff Hart asked, obviously not planning on believing a word of it.

"Eli Hunt."

15

Sheriff Hart didn't react to Leanne's declaration. He merely shook his head, like he'd expected as much, and turned his attention back to Dottie and me. "Go home, you two. I'm not in a forgiving mood, and you're pushing the boundaries of what I'm willing to ignore."

"I'm telling the truth," Leanne shouted.

The sheriff raised an eyebrow, his gaze meeting mine, challenging me. "I'm serious, Jo. Walk away."

"Don't you want to hear what she has to say?" I retorted, placing my hands on my hips. "You say you're just doing your job, but you're probably keeping Leanne in here because the rich Hollywood people are putting pressure on you. You want to prove you're doing something and making progress, but this isn't the way to do it."

Sheriff Hart's expression hardened, and I immediately knew I'd pushed him too far. Sheriff Hart was a good man who did his job well. It wasn't his fault that the evidence pointed to Leanne, whatever that evidence might be.

But it was his fault if he wasn't willing to listen to her.

"I'm sorry—" I started.

Sheriff Hart's hand shook as he raised it, like he was barely containing his anger. He pointed to the front door. "I've already had half the town bursting through that door, informing me why I can't have Leanne in that jail cell. Everyone assumes I have no good reason, like I arrested her for the fun of it, and I won't have you joining the throng, telling me I don't know how to properly do my job."

Dottie stood from her chair, then pulled on my arm. "He'll talk to Leanne and get the answers he needs," she whispered. "He'll do his job. But not with us hanging around."

She was right, of course. The sheriff didn't want us to have any more information than we already had—it would only encourage us.

We said our goodbyes, and as we left the sheriff's office, I turned to Dottie. "I messed up. I'm sorry. If I had known that the sheriff had installed security cameras and—"

Dottie held up a hand, stopping me. "We both know you've always been too curious for your own good, with a dash of impulsivity, and I could have said no." She paused. "I should have."

"You did say no," I said. "The night of the vigil." I could

see that Dottie was beating herself up about this, and I hated seeing her this way. "I always push and push and—"

We rounded the corner, and I stopped mid-step. There, on the sidewalk, in front of our bakery, was Eli Hunt.

Dottie glanced at me. "Why—" And then she saw what had caught my attention. Her gaze snapped back to me, accusatory.

I knew this looked bad, but this was obviously not my fault. Leave it to Dottie to think so highly of my skills that she thought I had telepathically called Eli Hunt and asked him to meet us for a secret rendezvous.

"Eli Hunt," Dottie said as we approached the bakery. She obviously didn't trust me to be the one to speak with him. "You heard about our pastries, did you?"

Eli Hunt turned to us. He wore an easy smile, but it seemed like the type that had been practiced so often, it had become second nature. Like it was meant for someone else but never for him.

"I have, yes. You're quite well known in your town." I knew the British accent was fake, but I still loved hearing it. "Someone mentioned you have beignets, and I've been craving them ever since." He tossed his smile my way. "I fell in love with beignets a couple years ago when I was traveling, but they are difficult to find."

"Ours are a little different than the ones you'd find in New Orleans," Dottie said, "but I think you'll like them all the same."

Eli stepped aside as Dottie unlocked the front door. "I

was introduced to them in Paris, actually. Rumor has it your pastry chef studied there."

Dottie paused, her hand still on the door handle. "It seems there have been a lot of rumors about our little bakery."

Eli Hunt may not have noticed the warning in Dottie's voice, but I had. Even though it was common knowledge that Autumn had studied in Paris, Dottie was worried that Eli had been talking to others about us—worried that our investigative tendencies may have been found out by the wrong people. As much as I liked Eli Hunt, I had to remember that he was still a suspect. Especially if Leanne was right and Eli really had picked up Blake Sommer from the community center.

That would make Eli Hunt the last person to see Blake alive.

Not me, as I had assumed.

"Well, don't just stand there," I told Dottie, as if nothing was wrong. "Invite the man in and offer him some beignets."

Eli gave me a grateful nod and then followed us inside. "Strange hours your bakery keeps," he said, taking in the small space.

"They're more stable during our busy season," I said. "I'll admit that I'm a bit distractable and I tend to wander off during the slow times. If folks want pastries, though, it's not hard to find us."

Eli didn't respond, his gaze lingering on the picture of

our eldest sister, Beatrice, holding a giant loaf of bread. Her photo was surrounded by tarot cards, a unique tribute to her life, but I knew she would have liked it.

"That's our sister," I said, stepping behind the counter. "She died a couple years ago."

Eli tore his gaze from it. "I'm sorry to hear that."

"No need," Dottie said, taking her place on one of the stools at the counter. "She was old."

Eli didn't seem to know whether he was allowed to laugh at the blunt statement, and his lips formed a tight line as he nodded, trying to keep it in.

Just as I took out a tray of beignets from the display case, Skittles sprinted into the room. She didn't so much as glance our way before leaping onto the counter.

"She's our mascot," I told Eli, shielding the beignets.

"Where's that cat?" Autumn yelled from the kitchen, storming into the room. Flour covered her from head to foot. "I swear, Dottie, if she jumps into my flour one more time, you're going to have to choose between keeping me or her. That's the second bag I've had to throw out today."

Skittles sensed the danger and leaped off the counter, then ran upstairs.

"And where were you two?" Autumn said, turning on Dottie and me. "You're supposed to tell me when you close up the bakery. I was baking as if we were going to sell out. Now we have way more than we need."

I cleared my throat and nodded to our customer. To his credit, Eli tried to look like he wasn't listening in on the conversation, intently studying the beignets I had pulled from the display case. Of course, no one could help but eavesdrop the way Autumn was yelling.

When Autumn turned and saw Eli Hunt standing in our bakery, her words died on her lips and her angry expression gave way to panic. And then embarrassment.

"Why didn't you stop me?" she whispered, her cheeks now a deep shade of red.

"We know a lost cause when we see it," Dottie said, not bothering to lower her voice.

That only increased Autumn's embarrassment.

Eli stepped back from the display case, and his gaze landed on Autumn. He pretended he'd just noticed her. "So, you must be the famous pastry chef I've heard so much about."

Autumn stared, only managing a brief "Mm-hm."

"Any chance I can get two dozen beignets?" he asked. "And anything else you baked too much of. I'm always looking to support a good cause." He said it with a slight smile, as if most people wouldn't consider buying way too many pastries a good cause.

Autumn was still too stunned to speak, so I returned his smile and pulled out a box from beneath the counter. "Two dozen beignets coming right up." I glanced at Autumn. "Do you have any recommendations for other pastries he might like?"

More silence. Dottie poked Autumn, and that seemed to do the trick.

"I have about ten thousand cream puffs in the back, if you want those," she said, giving a forced smile.

Eli Hunt leaned against the counter. "Cream puffs sound amazing, but instead of a thousand, let's make it five dozen. I want to give them to the film crew—you know, boost morale and that kind of thing."

I frowned. "You can't seriously be saying you'll continue shooting the movie after everything that has gone on."

Eli hesitated, and his smile dipped. "I hope to, eventually. But no, right now our screenwriter is sitting in a jail cell and another screenwriter is dead. Our entire crew is under investigation, and even though the sheriff arrested Leanne Warner, he's made sure we know we're all under suspicion. Hence the need for cream puffs to boost morale."

I nodded, thinking.

If it was incomprehensible to me that filming would continue after two deaths, it had to be just as incomprehensible to the killer. When one explosion wasn't enough to stop film production, another body had dropped. This time it had to be enough.

But who would be so desperate for the movie to be scrapped? Other than Frederick.

Not Leanne—she couldn't be the one who had shot Frederick. She might not have liked him, but this was her debut as a screenwriter, and she wouldn't have done anything to jeopardize that.

"Let's say that Blake's and Frederick's deaths aren't solved in the next few days," I said. "What will happen then?"

Eli Hunt raised a shoulder. "We'll all pack and go home and wait for this to be over." A pause. "With the sheriff's blessing, of course. Then maybe we could resume filming."

"So, you think you'll still be able to finish your movie," Dottie said, studying the actor. She still didn't trust him. "Even with all the negative publicity that will surround the film."

Eli nodded. "If anything, the negative publicity will intrigue people and get them wanting to see the film. It's not ideal, of course, but I don't think it will hurt us. Besides, Leanne's script is full of heart and humor—and depth. Nowadays, that combination has been in short supply in Hollywood."

"I'm so happy to hear that two murders are no match for Hollywood tenacity," Dottie said, bitterness lacing her words.

Eli's lips parted in surprise. "I didn't mean—"

"Yes, you did." Dottie folded her arms and glared. "I hear people talking. One of the victims was a nobody—no family and no one to miss him. The other victim—he was feared and hated, and most people aren't surprised by his death. They think he had it coming. You'll have no problem bouncing back from this little hiccup on your path to furthering your career."

Eli's gaze dropped, a mixture of emotions crossing his features.

After an extended silence, Autumn said, "I'll box up those cream puffs for you," and then disappeared into the back.

"It's not true," Eli finally said, looking up. "About either of them."

"We know it," I said, my voice soft. And then I waited for him to continue. I could tell there was something weighing heavily on Eli's mind, and the quieter I was, the better chance of him sharing it.

Eli was quiet for a long minute before finally shaking his head in frustration. "Frederick caused so many headaches over the last week, and yet he did recognize Leanne's talent. I wish people could have seen that side of him—the one that prompted him to take Leanne under his wing in the first place. He was her mentor, you know."

Not the victim I had hoped Eli would talk about, but I'd take it. For now.

"Then why was he trying to take over her screenplay?" I asked, handing Eli his boxes of beignets. "He was trying to push her out—take credit for what she'd done."

Eli released a long sigh and rubbed his face. "It's difficult for someone to admit when their season is over. Frederick has seen the end coming for quite some time, which is the only reason he became a mentor in the first place. Leanne would be his protégée who would pick up the mantle. However, I think the reality of it struck him differently when I purchased her screenplay, and it was more difficult to let go than he'd anticipated." A pause. "I know how it looks. Frederick could be intense—mean, even. But all in all, he was a good man, and he didn't deserve to die."

Eli Hunt certainly wasn't speaking like a killer.

"And what about Blake Sommer?" Dottie said. "Did his past mistakes warrant his death?"

Eli's expression slackened, and he momentarily lost his grip on the pastry box he held. Luckily, he had fast reflexes and caught the box before it fell. "What do you know about Blake's past?"

16

Judging by Eli's reaction, Frederick had been right.

"The more important question," Dottie said, sliding off her stool, "is why you didn't tell the sheriff about it. That won't look good for you when he finds out."

We knew nothing about Blake's past except what Frederick had told us, but Dottie was treating it as if we knew everything. She was bluffing, hoping that Eli would reveal more to us than we already knew. I knew the tactic well— she'd used it on me many times when we were teenagers.

I'd hated it. Mostly because nine times out of ten, it had worked.

"I didn't think it was relevant," Eli said, looking panicked. His English accent seemed thicker than it had a moment ago, like he was trying to hide behind it. "I hadn't seen Blake since we were kids, not for lack of trying. But I had no idea where they had sent him, and no one would tell me. I always hoped a miracle would happen and one day I'd find him."

"Do you still blame yourself?" I asked, my voice quiet.

Eli hesitated. "I know it's stupid—I shouldn't blame myself. But it's difficult when I became a world-famous actor and my brother became a criminal. Those roles could have easily been reversed. What if he had been the one to be adopted instead?" Eli's gaze met mine. "How did you know Blake was my brother? No one knows that."

I shrugged, not wanting Eli to know that we hadn't known they were brothers.

Before now, I hadn't considered Frederick the most reliable source, and it did make me wonder how the screenwriter had known such an intimate detail about the actor's former life.

"It wasn't your fault," I said instead. "You were just kids."

Eli slumped onto a stool at the display case. "We were, but it didn't feel like it at the time. I begged our foster parents to adopt Blake. It's difficult to find someone to adopt older kids—I was fourteen and he was eleven at the time, and I knew that he'd likely never be adopted if they sent him to a new foster home.

"But Blake—he wasn't easy to love. He kept all his pain locked away, and he wouldn't let anyone in. Except me." He paused. "Our foster parents were never able to see that side of him. Instead, he pushed them away. Didn't trust them not to leave us like our own parents had."

"You two went through a lot," I said. "That had to be hard on you when he was sent to a different home."

Eli gave a humorless laugh. "I cried for weeks, begging them to take him back. I told them he wouldn't steal anymore and he'd be good, but they didn't listen. Before they adopted me, I thought they were the kindest, most wonderful people on the planet. But I never forgave them for turning their backs on Blake."

"It seems you weren't able to forgive yourself either," I said.

Eli's gaze dropped. "Right when I was starting to become famous, my agent forwarded an email to me. Blake hadn't known how else to get in touch with me. He wanted to meet up for lunch and talk. Reconnect."

"And did you?" I asked.

From the way Eli had said it, I knew they hadn't.

Eli shook his head sadly. "I had such a strict schedule and felt I had to be everywhere I was asked to go and do everything exactly how I was told. I knew how difficult getting into this business was." His gaze pleaded with us—begging us to understand. "I was on the brink of something amazing, and I didn't want to do anything to mess it up. I offered to fly him out to New York when I finished filming the movie I was working on, but he took that to mean that my movie meant more to me than he did. He didn't answer. Just disappeared again."

"I don't blame him," Dottie said. "His family gave him

away, his brother became famous, and once again it was reaffirmed that he didn't matter."

Eli looked like he wanted to protest, but then his lips pressed into a straight line. "You're right," he finally said. "My own brother felt like he needed to sneak onto one of my sets as a background actor in order to talk to me—to spend time with me. No wonder he hated me."

I tilted my head to the side. "Hated you enough to try to sabotage your debut as a producer?"

Eli looked uncomfortable at the question and stepped away from the counter. He glanced at his phone, as if he was just realizing the time. "If I could get those cream puffs, I really should be getting back."

As if on cue, Autumn appeared with a large bag filled with several boxes. "Got everything right here." As she handed Eli the bag, she hesitated, as if she wanted to say something but was unsure if she should.

"Oh, for heaven's sake, just ask him for the photo," Dottie said, her lips twitching up in amusement.

Surprise flashed across Eli's face, like the thought hadn't even occurred to him. "Would you like a picture with me?"

Red crept into Autumn's cheeks, but she gave a little nod. "If it's not too much trouble."

A smile erupted across his face, and he looked like his usual confident self, as if he hadn't just told us about his tragic life story and insinuated that his brother could have blown up Christopher's trailer—and like Eli had dismissed the idea as crazy.

He placed the bag of pastries on the counter, alongside his credit card, and Autumn handed me her phone.

"You need to tell the sheriff everything," Dottie said as soon as the picture had been taken. "And the longer you wait, the worse it will look for you."

Autumn stepped behind the counter and rung up his purchase. After she'd returned his card, he gave a nod and picked up the pastries. "I know. And I hope you believe me when I say that the day my adoptive parents sent Blake to a new foster family was the worst day of my life. It's like you said, though, I was a kid. What could I have done?"

He didn't seem to expect an answer and quickly left the shop.

Dottie and I watched him walk away, then I released a long sigh.

"I don't think he did it."

Dottie glanced at me. "Why, because he told us a sad story? Maybe the man couldn't have done much about the situation when they were young, but he's had plenty of time to make amends. I think he was only interested in reconnecting with his brother if it was convenient—and then Blake showed up here. Eli couldn't have his long-lost brother messing up his career."

I could see where she was coming from, but the way he'd looked so heartbroken as he'd told his story, I just couldn't believe he'd kill his brother. "Eli would have known that a death on his movie set wouldn't be good for his career either," I pointed out. "And what about Frederick? You think Eli killed him too?"

Dottie shrugged. "What if Frederick witnessed the whole thing? Maybe that's how he knew about Eli and Blake's past. Eli could have been paying Frederick to keep quiet. But Frederick knew what he'd done, and he'd always be a threat. So, the screenwriter had to go."

"I don't buy it," I said.

"Eli wouldn't have wanted another death on set, of course, but he was desperate." Dottie waved a hand toward the door. "You saw how he talked about his brother. There was no emotion there—heck, he never broke character, just talked in that British accent the whole time. Eli couldn't care less about Blake."

"Too much time had passed," I protested. "They no longer had a relationship. You don't think it's weird that Blake suddenly emailed Eli and popped back into his life when he was starting to become famous? Eli probably thought his brother was only interested in his money. And who knows, maybe that was the reality of the situation."

"We'll never know, because Blake is dead."

Autumn had quietly been cleaning behind the counter but set down the rag she was holding. "What does Sheriff Hart think about it?"

Both Dottie and I looked at her. It had been a quiet reminder that this was not our problem to solve and we needed to tell the sheriff what we knew. Anything to help point him in a direction that wasn't Leanne. She and Isaac had a wedding to plan and a business to run, after all, and her being in jail put a damper on things.

"I guess we better find out," I said. "I'll get the cat. Autumn, you get the leash."

I was fairly certain we'd pushed the sheriff past his limit today, and when he found out what we knew and how we'd gotten that information, we'd need Skittles' cuteness to shield us from anything coming our way.

17

As I had expected, when Dottie and I walked into the sheriff's office, he was not pleased to see us. I had hoped to only need to use Skittles in case of an emergency, but the moment the sheriff's lips dipped into a frown, I scooped her up and held her so she and the sheriff could make eye contact.

"We decided to take Skittles on a walk, and she seemed particularly eager to come visit you," I said. "There's something about this office that calms her—I can tell she trusts you. Would you like to hold her?"

And then I forced her into his arms before he could stop me.

I'd expected Skittles to be annoyed at me and immediately jump from the sheriff's arms, but she instead settled in against his chest, like she had understood the assignment. She even threw in some purring for good measure.

The sheriff now looked somewhere between frustrated and bewildered.

"While the two of you are getting acquainted, may I see your keys to the jail cell?" I asked. "Leanne has a bed and breakfast to run—something that Isaac could normally help out with, but he still has a month left in that wheelchair of his. And then there is the movie that Leanne is still needed for, and a wedding to plan. It really is too much, but some people are built to be busy. I've never been that way myself, however it's a quality I admire in others." I held out a hand, ready to accept his keys.

Sheriff Hart didn't move to hand them to me, but of course, his arms were full.

I'd gotten the order of operations wrong—I should have asked for the keys and then handed him the cat, though I doubted it would have been any more effective.

Sheriff Hart sputtered, looking from the cat to my sister and me.

Dottie released a long sigh. "I apologize, Sheriff. Jo is getting ahead of herself. We came to give you information that could help your case. We don't want any secrets between us, and we certainly don't want to be accused of meddling in your case." When the sheriff opened his mouth to speak, Dottie held up a finger, indicating that she wasn't finished. "We understand that you are very good at your job, and we don't want you to think that we went out seeking this information. It landed in our laps, so to speak."

After a long pause, Sheriff Hart lowered himself into his chair, careful to not disturb Skittles. I'd known the cat was a good idea.

"I feel like I'm being manipulated," he finally said. "I don't like that feeling. It makes me difficult to work with. And it makes it difficult for me to trust."

"The last thing we want you to feel is manipulated," Dottie said, stepping forward. "I can take the cat. Jo was just worried that you'd be angry with us when you discovered we had spoken with one of your suspects. But it wasn't our fault, truly."

When Dottie moved to take the cat from the sheriff's arms, Sheriff Hart leaned back and out of her reach. "She's half asleep. Maybe we should leave her alone for the time being."

Skittles' eyes had closed, and she was purring so loudly that I was sure Leanne could hear it from her cell across the room.

I bit back a smile, enjoying the image of Skittles nestled in the arms of our sheriff. They really did make a cute pair.

"If you insist," Dottie said, stepping back and trying to hide her smile.

The sheriff chose to ignore it and turned to me. "So, what is the information you accidentally stumbled on—apparently through no fault of your own?"

I caught Dottie's eye, hoping she'd understand that I wanted her to share the information. Sheriff Hart liked me, but he didn't trust me like he did Dottie. He saw my sister as a no-nonsense cop who valued honesty.

Me, on the other hand, well, he'd had to arrest me after I'd stolen evidence a couple of years back, so there was that.

Thankfully, we had sister telepathy, and she gave a subtle nod before turning back to the sheriff.

"We don't know how, or if, this information is new to you, or if it will help with your investigation," Dottie started. "But Blake Sommer was only obsessed with Eli Hunt because they were estranged brothers. They'd been given up for adoption when Eli was fourteen, but Blake never made it out of foster care."

The sheriff's lips parted in surprise. Guess the information was new after all.

"And you think Blake was out for revenge against his famous brother?" Sheriff Hart asked, stroking Skittles' head. It was in a thoughtful way, like it was helping him process the information.

"We don't know why Blake was here," Dottie said. "I do think he was resentful toward his brother, but I think it's more likely he was here for money. It seems to me that he felt his brother owed him for all the years Eli had in a stable home—an opportunity that Blake did not receive."

"Due to Blake being a petty thief by the time he was eleven years old," I added.

Sheriff Hart nodded slowly. "So, you think it was Eli who killed his brother—he wasn't about to let his past come back to haunt him, let alone allow Blake to demand money from him."

"That depends," I said. "If we say yes, will you release Leanne from your jail cell?"

The sheriff looked like he wanted to laugh, but he did a very good job of keeping it under control. "I'm sorry, Jo, but this isn't enough. Not when Leanne's prints were found on the weapon that killed Frederick. Your information tells me I need to consider Eli Hunt a suspect in his brother's death—it doesn't tell me that he also killed the screenwriter."

I stared. "Leanne's prints were on the gun that killed Frederick?"

Oh, this wasn't good. Two murders really did complicate things. Why couldn't we have just one at a time like a normal town?

"Did we just get Eli Hunt arrested for murder while not helping Leanne out at all?" I whispered to Dottie.

She swallowed hard. "I do believe that's what the sheriff is saying. Yes."

"Did you have anything else you needed to share with me?" Sheriff Hart asked, adjusting his position in the chair. Likely, his legs had fallen asleep by now. Skittles didn't appreciate the sudden movement and leaped from his lap. The sheriff looked both disappointed and relieved. I knew the feeling well.

I didn't dare say anything more. We'd come here out of

a sense of duty and wanting to do the right thing, and we'd only made things worse.

"That was it," I said, grabbing Skittles' leash.

Sheriff Hart looked like he didn't know whether he should believe me, but he didn't stop us as we left.

"We need to come back and talk with Leanne when the sheriff isn't there," I murmured as we exited the station. "I'll pack up some beignets. Maybe then she'll forgive us for making a mess of things."

"If you want to bring her some pastries to help lift her spirits, that's fine," Dottie said. "But we are not going to sneak back here at night, and we're certainly not going to interrogate her behind the sheriff's back."

"Oh, all right, if you insist," I said.

Dottie's eyebrows immediately popped up, and I realized my mistake. I was never that agreeable and should have argued a bit more before giving in.

Dottie didn't push it, though, and we managed to finish the walk home without someone dying or us confronting any murder suspects. That was progress.

I EASED OPEN the back door of the bakery and motioned for Autumn to follow me out. She'd initially been hesitant about going along with my plan, but I'd managed to convince her that it was the only way we'd be able to help Leanne. And frankly, I didn't want to do it alone.

"Dorothy is not going to be happy if she finds out we went without her," Autumn whispered. She was wearing all black—something I told her not to, it only looked suspicious—but it seemed she thought we were in a spy movie. And she was a spy who was carrying a box of beignets that had a pink bow tied around the middle.

I, on the other hand, was wearing my brightest blouse that was covered in orange flowers. The more we tried to stand out, the less we actually would was my reasoning.

"You brought extra beignets for Deputy Randy, right?" I asked as I eased the bakery door closed behind me.

"Of course," she said. "Got to keep him distracted while we talk with Leanne."

It was the equivalent of bringing meat to keep the guard dogs at bay. Except this guard dog had the personality of a golden retriever.

As we set out toward the boardwalk, I could see campfires dotting the beach. The sunset stroll.

I'd thought it would be over by now—it was late enough that Dottie had been in bed an hour already.

"What time is it?" I asked Autumn. "Do you think Leanne will still be awake?"

It was something I hadn't considered until now, and I worried it would be the downfall of this plan.

Autumn glanced at her phone, then released an amused snort. "Uh, yeah. Pretty sure she'll still be up."

"Why is that?"

"Because it's only eight-thirty."

Huh. I could have sworn it was later than that. This was good, though. Any later and our visit would be all the more suspicious, and yet it was late enough that the sheriff shouldn't be at the office.

"Just you wait until you're my age," I told Autumn. "Time goes topsy turvy on you. You'll be up at four-thirty every morning and in bed by seven. It doesn't seem fair sometimes because I miss all the good stuff, but there you have it."

Autumn laughed. "That's already my schedule. I have to be at work by five every morning, remember? I'm so exhausted by the time I get home that I'm not in bed much later than you are."

I stopped mid-step, horrified. "I'm sorry. It never occurred to me. I can't believe we have done that to you. To think we're robbing you of the best years of your life. It's unforgivable."

Autumn gave an amused shake of her head. "Really, it's not a big deal. I'm a morning person and—"

I raised a hand, interrupting her. "No, I'm sorry, but I can't in good conscience allow this to continue. We will be opening two hours later from now on—you don't have to be at the bakery until seven."

"But that means you won't open until twelve," she protested. "That's far too late."

We weren't able to come to a resolution before arriving at the sheriff's office. The moment it came into view, we both stopped in our tracks—not only was Sheriff Hart still at the office, but he was escorting a handcuffed woman into the building.

"It's too dark for me to see her face," I muttered, feeling particularly grumpy about my age this evening. "Could you see who it was?"

"No, sorry," Autumn said. "It's too dark for anyone to see that far. Besides, her back was turned to us."

Well, that at least made me feel a little better.

"Do you think this means he's released Leanne?" I asked, hopeful.

"I doubt it," Autumn said. "He probably put them in there together."

I frowned. "But there's only one cot in there. We should confront him for cruel and unusual punishment."

Autumn smiled. "I'm sure they'll be fine. Sheriff Hart took good care of you, didn't he?"

Her smile immediately dipped, and her eyes were anxious, like she was wondering if she'd crossed a line by mentioning the time I'd been arrested. I was fairly certain that Autumn was still traumatized from the whole ordeal.

"That's true," I said. "But I'm also an old woman, and that makes a difference. Randy brought in an entire mattress and boxspring for me—I doubt those two women will be able to pull that off."

Autumn's lips twitched back up.

Good. A happy Autumn was a happy bakery.

My gaze shifted back to the sheriff's office, and I let out

a disappointed sigh. "There's no way we can visit Leanne now—the sheriff would arrest us for even trying."

Autumn held up the box she was carrying. "Not if we have pastries." And then she marched forward toward the sheriff's office.

I was fairly certain this was a bad idea, even by my standards, but there was no way I could tell Autumn that.

I had a reputation to keep.

18

The sheriff's office was quiet when we entered. Maybe our luck had turned. I motioned for Autumn to follow me, then began walking on my toes, hoping we could get in and out without the sheriff ever realizing we had been there.

That got tiring after three or four steps, so I resolved to merely walk quietly.

However, as we turned to the left and made our way to Leanne's cell, I saw that the sheriff was already there. And Jennifer was there with him.

She didn't look at all like a suspect, though. No handcuffs, like I swore I'd seen.

I stopped and attempted to retreat without being noticed, but it was too late. Both the sheriff and Jennifer turned, and neither of them seemed pleased to see us.

Autumn gave me a questioning glance, assuming I had

a plan to get us out of this pickle. When I grimaced, she realized I had no idea what I was doing, so she turned back to the sheriff and raised the pastry box.

"Beignet?" she said, though the words were weak and far from convincing anyone that we were the innocent ones in this situation.

I had seen Sheriff Hart angry before, but this was a whole new level. The vein in his forehead pulsed, and the ones in his neck seemed to pop out.

The sheriff didn't say a thing, however, but merely unlocked the cell door, opened it wide, then motioned for me to go inside.

"I can see that we came at a bad time," I said, taking a step backwards. "We only wanted a chance to visit Leanne and give her some pastries—something to cheer her up. But they'll still be good tomorrow."

Sheriff Hart didn't move. "Jo, get inside."

I crossed my arms defiantly and said, "No. I'm not under arrest, and I know my rights."

Sometimes I didn't know when I had the losing hand, and this was one of those times.

Sheriff Hart knew me better than I wished he did, and he turned to Autumn.

"I want the truth, Autumn. Did you bring the pastries so you could question Leanne about what happened on set when Frederick was murdered?"

Autumn threw a panicked glance my way.

Oh, Sheriff Hart was good. He knew Autumn was terrified of him and she'd never dare lie.

"Yes, sir," she said, and then mouthed to me, "I'm sorry."

I gave her a smile so she'd know I didn't fault her. It was me who had gotten us into this situation—Dottie had been right to stay out of it.

The sheriff turned back to me. "You've been warned several times over the last few days, Jo. That means you have wandered into obstruction of justice territory." He nodded again to the cell. "Let's go."

I had one more play left in my book.

"There's only one cot," I said. "If I have to sleep on the hard floor, I'll likely die before I can get back up again. That's murder."

Sheriff Hart seemed unfazed by this and merely smiled. It was unsettling. "Lucky for you I have a couple extra cots in the back—I got them on sale. I'll have Randy retrieve one for you." He paused. "I hate to be the bearer of more bad news, but he won't be getting you a mattress this time. A cot is the best we can do."

He didn't look at all sorry for it.

I knew the sheriff liked me, and most times I could tell. It was in the little things he would do—and last time he'd arrested me, he really had looked sorry for it.

Something was different right now, though, and for the first time since we'd met, I began to wonder if his fondness for me had worn off. Maybe I had pushed too hard and I'd been more than he could handle.

It wouldn't be the first time I'd done that with someone.

But then something occurred to me, and I suddenly wasn't all that sorry to be spending the night in jail.

I glanced back at Autumn. "Don't tell Dottie what has happened until you come in for work tomorrow morning —let her sleep."

Autumn looked like she wanted to protest, but I held up a finger. "My situation isn't going to be different either way, except if you wake her up tonight, you'll then be dealing with tired and cranky Dottie, and is that what you really want?"

Autumn's lips pursed in annoyance, because she knew I was right. "You know I don't."

I gave a satisfied nod and took a step toward the cell before I remembered something. I turned back and took the box of pastries from Autumn's arms. "I'm going to need these."

And then I shuffled into the cell, mostly to make the sheriff feel bad about putting an elderly woman in jail when she'd done nothing wrong except try to help.

Sheriff Hart seemed completely unaffected by it—it seemed he'd managed to build an immunity to my elderly ways.

Well, that was one less tool in my belt. Thankfully, I had others.

Jennifer had been standing off to the side, watching the exchange with a bewildered expression. "I'm sorry, but why is Jo being arrested?" she asked as the sheriff shut the door and locked it.

I had to say, the last cell I'd been in had been much more comfortable than this one. But I supposed beggars couldn't be choosers.

"Because she's been impeding my investigation from the very start, like always." He put his keys in his pocket and turned away. "It needs to stop, and it seems that this is the only language Jo Darby understands."

I gave Jennifer a smile so she'd know there were no hard feelings against the sheriff. "The real question, dear, is why you are here. The sheriff isn't putting you in here too, is he? It seems he has enough cots for the three of us."

Jennifer glanced at the sheriff, looking suddenly nervous, like the thought hadn't occurred to her and she was seeking confirmation that she was not, in fact, being arrested.

Sheriff Hart shook his head. "No, not at all. Routine questioning. Jennifer was on set at the time of Frederick's murder."

She looked relieved at this news, and her smile returned. "I'm happy to help in any way I can."

"Aren't we all," I said, giving the sheriff a pointed look. He refused to meet my gaze. My attention returned to Jennifer. "And your friends, are they all set to head home tomorrow? I'm sorry it didn't turn out the way they'd hoped. Hopefully they at least got an autograph or two."

Jennifer's smile dipped, her anxiety returning. "Um, yes, Eli was very kind in that regard."

Sheriff Hart seemed skeptical of my line of questioning, probably because he suspected I was up to something, and he cleared his throat. "Right. Well, I believe it's time for Miss Cole and me to finish our business elsewhere." He nodded for her to follow him, and she gave me a little wave.

"Good luck," she whispered, and then hurried after the sheriff, who was already halfway across the station and motioning for her to follow him outside. It seemed he really didn't want me speaking with Jennifer.

"I wonder why she's really here," I mused as I looked around my new accommodations. "And when Randy is coming with that cot."

Leanne sat on one end of her cot, then patted it, inviting me to join her. "He was called out to the sunset stroll, but that's not surprising. Apparently, he's been called out there every evening since filming started." She wore a guilty expression, but I didn't see how that was her fault.

"You can't blame yourself," I said.

"I knew that Starlight Ridge would be the perfect place for this movie to be filmed, and I'm the one who suggested it to Eli, but I forgot about the toll it would have on the community," she said. "The film crew and actors... They're big-city people. And they act like it."

"Like I said, it's not your fault," I said. "People are who they are."

"True," Leanne said. "I think what people are most frustrated by is not being able to hang any Christmas decorations on Main Street, in the middle of December." She paused. "That and the murders."

"Yes, the murders certainly have put a damper on things," I said, easing myself onto the cot. I really wished I had some back support about now. "Have you noticed people always wait until they come on vacation in our town to do their murdering? And we get blamed for it. Why can't they murder people back at home? It would certainly make our lives easier."

Leanne glanced toward the front door, then lowered her voice, even though the sheriff was no longer in the station. "Between me and you, I wouldn't be surprised if Jennifer will be in this cell before midnight. That's the real reason the sheriff's talking to her—because he thinks she did it. Or at least knows who did."

I couldn't hide my surprise at Leanne's bold declaration. "I hardly think she's the type. Besides, what motive did she have?"

"The sheriff got a phone call earlier this afternoon," Leanne said, keeping her voice at a whisper. "I could only hear one side of the conversation, of course, but after he hung up, the sheriff sounded upset. He told Randy that

Jennifer had snuck two men onto set—two screenwriters. And they had been harassing Christopher. The thing is, and I told the sheriff this, I saw it with my own two eyes. It was on at least two occasions that I saw them pestering Christopher to read their script. Of course, he doesn't have time for a thing like that right now, and he's already told me that he wants to work with me on future projects. There isn't room for another screenwriter, let alone two."

I didn't need to ask who it was that had called the sheriff.

"Oh, darn it, Dottie," I mumbled.

I hadn't mean to say it out loud, and Leanne was looking at me with a curious expression. I supposed she'd find out sooner or later—you could hear everything in this station, which was the reason I'd chosen to not fight the sheriff and instead sit in this cell. Because Leanne had been quietly gathering up all sorts of information over the past day—information she may not have even realized was valuable.

"It had to have been Dottie who called the sheriff and told him about Jennifer and her friends," I admitted. "They confided in us earlier about trying to get noticed by the director. They were worried the sheriff would suspect them of the murders because they were the only ones who weren't supposed to be here. Dottie must have been feeling guilty after a particularly unpleasant conversation we had with the sheriff, and called him to let him know everything we had been told. She'd rather die than be accused of impeding an investigation."

Leanne nodded. "That makes sense, though I don't know why he brought Jennifer over here to talk to me. He didn't get a chance to say much before you and Autumn arrived."

"Probably to see if you two showed any reaction to seeing each other," I said. "If you were working together, there could be some panic or avoidance."

Leanne gawked. "Me and Jennifer working together to kill two people? That's the most ridiculous thing I've ever heard."

"Ridiculous or not, you could come and go without raising suspicion. Same with Jennifer. Your fingerprints were on the gun, and Jennifer had sneaked two friends onto set. They'd even visited the director in his trailer."

"Unbelievable," Leanne said, rubbing her eyebrows. "Isaac was arrested for murder several months ago, and now me, both of us supposedly involved in high-profile murders. I'm sure the media is on their way back to Starlight Ridge now, the vultures that they are. My career as a screenwriter is over. Good thing I have the bed and breakfast."

I wondered who was running the bed and breakfast while Leanne was here. Isaac was still in his wheelchair, so I wasn't sure how much help he could be.

"Is there someone at the bed and breakfast helping manage things?" I asked.

Leanne nodded. "My sister, Jules."

Well, at least there was that.

My mind wandered back to something Leanne had said. These murders were high profile, and the media would be back. All it took was one person trying to get a quick payday by leaking information about Frederick's death.

That meant the pressure was rising, and whenever that was the situation, Sheriff Hart tended to arrest people more quickly.

It wasn't his fault; it was human nature. If powerful people weren't satisfied with the progress being made, they just kept coming back harder and stronger. I didn't blame the sheriff one bit for trying to get them off his back.

"Is Christopher pressuring the sheriff to get this resolved quickly?" I asked Leanne.

Leanne hesitated but then nodded. "Yes, and it's understandable why. We were able to continue filming after Blake's death, but now that the chocolate shop is a crime scene, if these murders aren't resolved within the next couple days, Christopher is going to have to pull out and send everyone home."

"Wrapping up the investigation quickly would also help any fallout with the media," I mused. "If Christopher is able to tell them what happened and who Frederick's murderer is, there's no room for speculation."

"Exactly." Leanne scooted back on the cot and rested against the brick wall. That was an excellent idea, and even though it took a lot to scoot myself back, I managed to do the same.

"Do you really believe that Jennifer and her friends killed Blake and Frederick?" I asked Leanne. "You know Jennifer better than I do, but she hardly seems capable."

"I don't know," Leanne said, raising a shoulder. "I only know Jennifer in a professional capacity. This is the first time I've worked with her."

I nodded but didn't say anything. I didn't know what to think anymore, my mind twisted up into knots, unable to decipher what was important and what wasn't. I did not envy the sheriff's job.

"Do you think it's a possibility that the two murders are unrelated?" I asked.

Leanne hesitated. I could tell the question made her uncomfortable, and I was about to retract it when she answered.

19

Leanne gave me a long look. "The sheriff does think he's looking for two different people," she finally said. "The first murder seemed sloppy and unplanned, while the second murder was more calculated."

"He's pegged Jennifer or one of her friends for the first murder, and you for the second," I guessed.

Leanne nodded. "Unfortunately, yes, I believe that's how he sees it."

"But I didn't ask what the sheriff thinks," I said. "I want to know what you think."

Leanne had been sitting here all day with nothing to do but eavesdrop, so she had to know something.

But then I realized why Leanne was having such a difficult time with the question—she was a good person. And discussing who could be a murderer wasn't in her nature.

She was okay telling me who the sheriff thought it could be, but to accuse them herself—that felt different.

"It's okay, you don't have to answer," I said.

Leanne cut me off with a shake of her head before I could say more. "It's not that I don't want to, but I truly have no idea. As much as I like everyone on set, I'd much prefer that whoever it was be in this cell instead of me." She released a long sigh. "The thing is that Sheriff Hart has had so many people in here today, I don't know what's up or down anymore. It's not like anyone waltzed in and announced that they had killed two people, and everyone both has an alibi and seems suspicious at the same time."

"Who all has spoken with the sheriff?" I asked, not having realized how busy the sheriff had been. If he had been interviewing that many people—even now he was still questioning people—it must mean he didn't think that Leanne had murdered the two victims. Right now, he was working late because he was doing everything in his power to discover who it had really been.

It almost made me sorry that I had made his job harder. I couldn't be all the way sorry, though, because I had never intended to get involved with the investigation. I hadn't asked Jennifer and her friends to confide in Dottie and me. Had we followed them? Yes. But only because they'd been acting suspiciously—something that was hardly my fault. Any concerned citizen would have done the same.

"Everyone you could imagine has been in here today,"

Leanne said. "All the members of the film crew, Christopher, and Eli Hunt. Anyone who might know anything related to Blake Sommer or Frederick Alberheist."

"What about Jennifer's two screenwriter friends?" I asked. "Were they in here at all today?"

Leanne shook her head. "When Sheriff Hart sent Randy out to bring them in, he came back and said they'd skipped town."

It was a natural reaction for two people who thought they were about to be accused of murder, but not a smart one.

"I hope the sheriff doesn't waste his time going after them," I said. "They were nothing but two dumb kids who were trying to make all their wildest dreams come true. They shouldn't have left town, but it hardly makes them murderers."

"That's not what Christopher told Sheriff Hart," Leanne said. "He's saying that Jennifer's friends hounded him about their screenplay and were very upset with him when he turned them down."

I knew that to be true, but I still wasn't convinced.

"I suppose Christopher thinks that after they gave up on him, they tried showing their screenplay to Frederick. Maybe he'd mentor them the way he's mentored you."

Leanne glanced my way. "Yup. And you know how abrasive Frederick was. If they were angry enough to blow up Christopher's trailer, surely they could have been angry enough to kill Frederick."

I hesitated. "And what about you, Leanne? How on earth did your fingerprints end up on the gun that was used to kill him?"

Leanne's gaze dropped. "I was at the chocolate shop, using the display counter as a table, working on a couple last-minute rewrites." She pulled in a shuddered breath. "The shot came from back in the kitchen, where Adeline makes her chocolates—I hadn't realized anyone was even there. Adeline had said in no uncertain terms that that area of the store was off limits." Her gaze lifted and met mine. "I leaped from my seat and ran back there. That was when I saw Frederick lying on the floor. I hurried over to him, wanting to try to stop the bleeding, but when I knelt down next to him, I landed on something hard. I reached under my knee to pick it up, not knowing it was the gun—I had to move it, that was all. Christopher ran into the kitchen, and there I was, holding it. The murder weapon."

"So Christopher thought you did it, told the sheriff, and here you are," I murmured.

Leanne shook her head. "Oh, no, Christopher believed me and told the sheriff someone else must have done it, but fingerprints are fingerprints. And no one else was there."

Oh, that was bad luck. Leanne had wanted to help Frederick, someone that no one liked, and she was instead being blamed for his murder.

"I wish there was something I could say that could help you feel better," I said.

"I'd say that you proving my innocence, like you did with Isaac, would be more than enough, but I suppose you're not in much of a position to do that right now." She gestured to the cell we sat in.

I smiled. "I'm in a better position than you think." A pause. "I'm very confused, though. No one saw what happened at the beach when Christopher's trailer exploded or the chocolate shop when Frederick was killed? How does that happen?"

Leanne shrugged. "On a movie set, no one is paying attention to anyone else. They have a job to do, and they are focused on that one thing. Before the explosion on the beach, everyone was prepping for the next scene. Jennifer was gathering the background extras so she could bring them down to set, and Eli and Christopher were going over some last-minute notes in the script. People reported hearing a pop followed by the explosion, but it was on the opposite side of the beach, and it seems that no one but Blake Sommer had been anywhere near the trailer. It wasn't much different with Frederick's death. People were running around, doing their jobs—they wouldn't have noticed if someone slipped back into the kitchen."

I had been in Adeline's kitchen and knew there was a back entrance. Whoever had done it could have easily snuck out and circled around the building.

My forehead crinkled as I struggled to concentrate.

"I know you were on set when Frederick died, but how

did you know what was happening on the beach just before the explosion? Were you on set that day as well?"

Had Leanne been on set then, she would have had to race across town to get to the bed and breakfast in time to serve everyone lunch. And she hadn't seemed the least bit rushed when we saw her.

"Oh, no," she said with an embarrassed smile. "This was just from listening in throughout the day."

"And everyone's timetables matched up?" I asked, frowning.

Leanne gave me a curious look. "Yes. Why?"

I pushed myself to my feet. "Because at least two people have lied today, and I don't think you're one of them."

And then I pulled a set of keys from my pocket and let myself out of the cell.

20

I glanced back at Leanne and tried not to laugh at the shock on her face.

"Well, are you coming?"

Her lips parted, as if she wanted to say something, but no words came out.

I gave her a patient smile. "To answer your question, I slipped the keys out of the sheriff's pocket before he left with Jennifer. The bars on this cell are much wider than should be allowed."

A laugh burst from Leanne, and she quickly covered her mouth, as if afraid the sheriff had heard. "I'm very impressed, Jo."

I waved a hand through the air like it was no big deal. "He always wears those nice pants with the shallow pockets, so it wasn't hard." I gestured toward the empty office. "You coming? Because Randy will show up with a second cot, and you may not want to be here when he does."

Leanne hesitated. "I better stay. It's one thing for you to escape, but I was arrested as a murder suspect. There's a difference."

She had a point. "Suit yourself." I shut the cell door behind me, but I left it unlocked and made sure that she saw. "Just in case you change your mind."

I turned from the cell and quietly made my way to Randy's desk. Thank goodness he still had a landline. I noticed his drawer was slightly ajar, and I pushed it shut before sitting down in his chair and pulled out the number I'd been given a couple days earlier. It had been for questions regarding my role as a background actor, but I thought it could probably be used for this as well.

I glanced at my watch. Eleven o'clock. She was likely already in bed, but this was important and I was willing to risk her annoyance.

Jennifer picked up on the first ring. It looked like I wasn't the only one up past my bedtime.

"Hi Jennifer, this is Jo Darby, the woman that Sheriff Hart arrested this evening."

A small laugh. "I know who you are, Jo."

"Right. I'm sorry to disturb you at this late hour, but there has been a break in the case, and I felt you deserved some good news. The sheriff is heading over to the chocolate shop first thing in the morning to finish gathering the evidence he needs, and once he concludes his investigation, it will no longer be a crime scene. I wouldn't be surprised if you were back on schedule as early as tomorrow afternoon."

Jennifer didn't sound the least bit groggy as she thanked me for keeping her updated. I had expected her to ask at least a few follow-up questions, but she hung up before I even had a chance to say goodbye.

I nodded in satisfaction for a job well done, then walked to the front door and eased it open. I couldn't see Sheriff Hart or Jennifer, nor could I hear them, so I slipped out and down the steps. Seeing that the coast was clear, I made my way down the street and around the corner, toward the chocolate shop.

I was hoping I'd get lucky and the door would be unlocked, but the more I thought about it, the less likely that seemed, considering it was a crime scene.

A woman could hope.

I was nearly to the shop when someone yelled my name, and I froze. I'd thought I'd get further than this before being noticed. But then I heard it again, and this time it was more like an angry whisper, like the person was trying to get my attention but also be quiet.

When I turned, I saw Autumn and Dottie hurrying toward me.

Great.

I frowned as I waited for them to reach me, then gave Autumn the stink eye. "I told you to wait until morning to tell Dottie."

"Can you imagine the panic she'd have had if she woke in the middle of the night to find you gone?" Autumn asked, her tone defiant. "I wasn't going to do that to her—I was here the last time you were arrested, and I saw what she went through. She had a right to know."

Autumn had a point, but that didn't mean I had to be happy about it.

"I'm grateful she told me," Dottie said. "I can't believe the sheriff let you go so fast, though. I thought for sure he'd keep you overnight."

"And you were on your way to convince him to let me come home?" I asked, love for my sister washing over me. "That's so sweet."

Dottie harrumphed, as if to tell me she was still upset with me for getting myself arrested in the first place. "Where are you going at this time of night?" she asked, taking in our surroundings. The sunset stroll had been finished for at least a couple of hours and the boardwalk had long been deserted. We were alone, the moon high above us. Dottie turned back, frowning. "Seriously, you were on your way to the crime scene? Have you learned nothing from all this?"

I grinned. "I've learned a lot, actually, which is why I'm going there."

Dottie didn't look the least bit tempted to ask what I'd learned and instead pointed in the opposite direction. "We're going home. Now."

"Be my guest," I said. "But if you do that, the murderer is going to get away with it all."

I had known the button to push, and I saw Dottie's hesitation.

"I suggest you call the sheriff, then," she finally said. "This is his crime scene, and you shouldn't be anywhere near it. He's already arrested you once tonight, and he won't hesitate to do it again."

"True," I said. "But he doesn't know what I know, and he's going to thank me when all this is over."

Dottie raised her eyes to the sky, like she didn't know what she was going to do with me. "Then tell him what you know. That's what a normal person would do. Besides, no one is even out right now, so I don't know what you're hoping to accomplish."

"Not yet," I said, raising a finger. "But this place is going to get pretty busy in the next few minutes. I understand if you don't want to stay with me, but you need to make a quick decision, because I need to get inside the chocolate shop before everyone arrives."

"Exactly how many people are you expecting?"

I didn't answer. I knew Dottie was conflicted, and this was the very reason I hadn't wanted Autumn to tell her I was in jail. I didn't want my sister to feel like she had to choose between her own personal values and me. But here, yet again, she was being forced into that decision.

"Go home, Dottie," I said, my voice soft. I was going to help my sister out and make the decision for her. "You don't need to be here. The sheriff will be here before too long."

Autumn cocked one eyebrow. "How do you know that?"

"Because I stole his keys and escaped from his jail cell, and then had a phone conversation loud enough for Leanne to hear, so he'll know that the evidence he needs is at the chocolate shop. I also still have his keys." I lifted my pocket and dropped it, making the keys jingle.

Dottie didn't know what to do with that information, but it looked like she might want to beat me over the head with it.

"I cannot believe you've managed to do this to me again," she mumbled as she stomped her way to the chocolate shop. She was so angry that she hadn't even bothered with her cane, just kept whacking things with it as she walked.

This was progress.

"Please go home, Autumn," I said when I saw that our baker was following us. "I really don't want you to be involved with this."

I had seen how debilitating her anxiety could be, and the last thing I wanted was to make things worse for her. Simple, everyday situations were enough to send Autumn into a panic attack. A dangerous situation like this would put her in bed for a month.

Autumn hesitated but then nodded. "All right. But you have to promise me that you'll be careful. Wait until the sheriff arrives before you do anything stupid." She didn't look like she wanted to but she reversed direction, heading back toward her home.

Well, that was one less thing I needed to worry about.

Dottie and I turned back toward the chocolate shop—and stared. I didn't know why she wasn't moving or saying anything, but I knew exactly why I was rooted to the spot.

I was scared.

There, I admitted it. Even Jo Darby got scared sometimes, and for some reason, having my sister with me made me even more nervous about what we might find on the set of *Amaretto*.

I was pretty sure I knew who to expect, but would the sheriff get there when he needed to? I had no idea. He had been right, I often waited until the last minute to tell him anything and then waited for him to save the day.

I was now rethinking that strategy.

"Think it's unlocked?" Dottie asked, breaking the silence.

"Probably not. They have a lot of expensive equipment in there," I said. "And it's a crime scene."

"But you want to try anyway." It was a statement, not a question.

"Yup."

We slowly walked toward the chocolate shop, and I placed a hand on the front doorknob.

It was locked, of course.

"Sheriff Hart wouldn't have left it unlocked," Dottie whispered.

"He's not the only one with a key," I whispered back.

Dottie placed her hands on the front window and peered in. "I don't see any movement."

"If someone is here, they are probably in the kitchen, where Frederick was killed, making sure they didn't leave any evidence for the sheriff to find."

Dottie stepped back. "Why didn't you call the sheriff and make sure he made it here before they find whatever they are looking for?"

I gave her a side glance. "Because I didn't want him to know I had escaped."

"That doesn't matter right now," Dottie said, exasperated. "You need to call him and not rely on whatever weird game you're playing where you talk to one person and then hope that three people down the line, he receives the message that you intended."

"I'm supposed to call him right now?" I asked. "With what phone? This is why I want one for my birthday next month, for times like this."

"Well, forgive me for hoping there wouldn't be any more times like this," Dottie retorted.

Unfortunately for us, since we had moved to Starlight Ridge, there had often been times like this.

I had stepped back to join my sister, wondering what we should do, when the front door opened, causing us both to scream.

"You were locked up in my cell, and yet I'm still not surprised to see you two here," Sheriff Hart whispered harshly, opening the door wide enough for us to step past him. "Hurry, get inside."

Dottie and I shared alarmed looks but then hurried in after the sheriff. I turned and shut the door behind us, ensuring it remained unlocked.

"How did you get here so quickly?" I asked. "I wasn't sure you'd return to your office in time for Leanne to give you the message."

Sheriff Hart's eyes narrowed. "What message? And do I even want to know how you got out of that cell?"

I rummaged in my pocket and pulled out his keys. "It's not my fault—it's a medical condition." And then I dropped his keys into his outstretched hand.

The sheriff looked like he had something to say about that but managed to restrain himself. "Never mind that. I was already here when Autumn called me and said there was an emergency at the chocolate shop. She didn't say more before she hung up, but I'm assuming she was worried about something you two were about to do."

Autumn. Of course.

"Yes, I think that's a safe assumption," Dottie said.

Sheriff Hart blew out a hard breath and shook his head. "Making sure you two don't get yourselves killed has become my full-time job."

"That wasn't my intention," I said. "I set it up so that

you and whoever killed Frederick would be here at the same time. I was being helpful."

Sheriff Hart stared. "What do you mean by that?"

"I mean that we should probably be quiet and hide, or else we're going to scare them off. Jennifer spread the message at least ten minutes ago."

The sheriff looked like he might strangle me, but instead he motioned for us to hide behind the display counter. "You're trusting one of my murder suspects to lead the killer here?" he whispered as he positioned himself in a dark corner by the back door.

I smiled at his mistake. "Oh, no. She didn't know she was helping me."

And then the front door opened.

I peered through the glass in the display counter, and my heart sank.

It was not at all who I had been expecting.

ottie and I sat still, huddling behind the glass as Eli Hunt walked quietly through the chocolate shop. My foot was beginning to fall asleep, and I shifted my position but lost balance, and my knee bumped into the case.

I froze, and so did Eli. He took his phone out of his pocket and turned on the flashlight, sweeping the beam across the room. Thankfully, he didn't see us.

Eli put the phone away and crept forward, but he hadn't gotten halfway across the room when the front door opened for a second time.

Christopher walked in with Jennifer close behind.

"Eli," Christopher said as the door shut and the light from his phone landed on the actor. "What are you doing here?"

"Couldn't sleep," Eli said, turning toward him and Jennifer. "You?"

Jennifer smiled. "We were just going over some changes for tomorrow's schedule and I realized I left my laptop here. I haven't been able to access it since the shop became a crime scene, but now that the sheriff has his killer, we figured it would be all right to retrieve that."

"Uh-huh." Eli didn't look convinced, but it didn't seem he'd be pushing the issue either.

A pause.

"I'll just run into the back really quick to grab my laptop," Jennifer said, stepping around Christopher.

Sheriff Hart chose that moment to step into Jennifer's path. She screamed, her panicked gaze bouncing around the room, as if she were wondering if anyone else was going to jump out at her.

"Sheriff," she said with a soft laugh when she recognized him. "You scared me. I thought you wouldn't be here until—" She stopped, realizing her mistake. "I won't bore you with the details."

He smiled. "I don't get bored easily. Why don't you tell me those details while I accompany you to get that laptop of yours? It's still a crime scene, after all."

She glanced back at Eli and Christopher with an innocent look that said, *I didn't know it was still a crime scene. Did you?*

"Oh, I was under the impression you'd closed your investigation," she said. "If I had known, I would have waited."

"It's interesting that all three of you were under the

impression that this was no longer a crime scene," the sheriff said. "And that you decided that midnight was the best time to visit. If I were you, I'd have waited until morning, or at least turned on a light or two." He held up a finger, as if to warn Jennifer that she shouldn't go anywhere quite yet, and walked over to the other side of the room, where he flipped on the lights.

I wished he would have warned me. The lights were so blinding, I was seeing spots for close to a minute.

Before my vision had cleared all the way, I heard one of the men—it sounded like Eli—say, "Is someone else here?"

Oh, right. I had forgotten the display case was glass, and the overhead lights had made my and Dottie's hiding spot unusable. From the sheriff's expression, he had forgotten as well.

I slowly stood up, my joints protesting all the while, then gave Dottie an arm to help her pull herself up. I gave a little wave. "It sure does seem to be a popular time around here, doesn't it? You get those late-night munchies, and not even police tape can stop you."

"Jo and Dottie," Sheriff Hart barked. "What have I told you about sneaking onto crime scenes? I know you see it as a hobby, but you've crossed the line one too many times."

He was pretending he hadn't realized we were there, and it was a very clever idea.

"Oh, come now, Sheriff, these two are merely inquisitive, and they don't deserve to be locked up like criminals," Jennifer said. "Besides, you already did that to Jo earlier and, from the looks of it, realized that's not where she belongs. I think it's great that she and Dottie have something they're interested in at their age. It's better than waddling around the house and watching TV all day."

"I don't waddle," Dottie said grumpily.

"And they don't watch TV," Sheriff Hart said. "They have a business to run, but it's closed half the time because they think they're Sherlock Holmes and Watson."

"I'm Sherlock," I said, lifting a finger.

Dottie rolled her eyes. "Do you have professional law enforcement training? No, I didn't think so. If anyone is Sherlock in this duo, it's me."

"But I'm always having to drag you along for the ride," I said. "You didn't even want to come here tonight."

"Wait, why are you here?" Eli interrupted. "It's a bit late for you two to be out on the town, and I'm assuming it wasn't for the chocolates."

"It's true, it is past my bedtime," Dottie said. "But as a matter of fact, I *am* here for the chocolates."

"Definitely here for the chocolates," I agreed. "And then there's the small matter of one or more of you being a killer."

Jennifer snorted. "That's preposterous."

I shrugged. "Maybe. But I called you and told you the sheriff would be visiting the crime scene in the morning to gather the evidence he needed to arrest the killer. That meant the killer would need to revisit the crime scene tonight if they wanted to make sure they hadn't missed anything." My gaze swept over Jennifer, Christopher, and Eli. "So, which one of you is it?"

Silence.

All three were frozen, eyeing each other in suspicion.

Interesting that these three people had worked with each other every single day but there wasn't an ounce of trust between them. Maybe this wasn't unusual for Hollywood, but I was grateful I didn't run my own life this way.

"It wasn't me," Jennifer finally said.

"Then why did you hurry over here the moment you heard I was going to be collecting the final evidence I needed?" Sheriff Hart asked, his gaze intense.

Jennifer's lips opened several times before she finally managed to speak. "I was worried about my friends. I can't account for their whereabouts for most of the time they were in town, and I got worried that there would be some sort of evidence that pointed in their direction. If they were responsible for the explosion, it would have been an accident—they are the sweetest guys you'll ever meet."

"Unless they're trying to get you to read their script," Christopher mumbled.

Jennifer shot him an annoyed look. "Anyway, maybe they panicked and that's why they left town so suddenly, or maybe they just saw that there was no way they were ever going to convince Christopher to read their script. But honest to goodness, they couldn't have done it. They weren't—"

"Maybe they did," Sheriff Hart interrupted, taking a

step toward her. "And maybe Frederick knew it. We found Frederick's lighter close to the debris, after all. And maybe he decided it would be fun to blackmail the two of them. And maybe you said you'd help them and clean up their mess—because they were such good guys."

"No, of course not," Jennifer spluttered, realizing she'd dug herself into a hole that she wasn't quite sure how to get herself out of.

I felt sorry for the girl.

"It wasn't her," I said, my voice quiet.

Sheriff Hart glanced at me, annoyed by the interruption. It seemed he'd just gotten started. "There's no way you could possibly know that."

I nodded. "True. I'm never a hundred percent sure about anything. But I do know that both Eli and Christopher lied to you today. You might want to start there, especially because they had a much closer connection to Frederick Alberheist and Blake Sommer than Jennifer or her friends did."

Sheriff Hart looked like he wanted to ask how I had any knowledge of his private conversations, but instead he turned back to the two men.

"Is that true? Did you lie to me?"

They shared uneasy glances.

"Yes, we did," Eli finally said. "But it's not Christopher's fault. I asked him to cover for me." He paused, as if mustering up the courage to tell the truth. "Just before the explosion, I was with Blake Sommer. We'd driven down to the beach together, wanting a few minutes away from all the craziness around here."

"Because he's your estranged brother," Sheriff Hart said, recalling the information I had told him earlier.

Eli seemed surprised that the sheriff knew this information. "Yes," he said slowly. "Well, you can see how that looks, and I confided in Christopher. He agreed to be my alibi for the time of the explosion, and we decided it made the most sense to say that we had been going over last-minute notes in the script. But I swear I wasn't responsible for the explosion, or for Frederick's death."

Sheriff Hart studied the man for a minute before asking, "If you and Blake were together, then how did your brother end up dying in that explosion, and you managed to get away unscathed?"

Eli's breath hitched. "I've hidden my past from the public, and from everyone I worked with. I didn't think it was any of their business." He glanced at me, most likely thinking of our earlier conversation. His eyes were questioning, asking if I'd spilled all his secrets. When I didn't give any indication either way, he turned back to the sheriff. "I wanted to introduce Blake to Christopher, as a peace offering. I wanted to show my brother that I wasn't ashamed of him. I had heard that Christopher might be in his trailer—someone had seen him walking that way—and I parked my car on the boardwalk."

"Once again," Sheriff Hart said, his patience wearing thin, "why was he at the trailer and you weren't?"

"Because a fan stopped me and asked me for a photograph, and I obliged. I told Blake I'd meet him at the trailer." His gaze dropped. "I was ready to introduce Blake to Christopher, but I wasn't ready to introduce him to the world. And I've been beating myself up about it ever since."

"That's so sad," I said, my voice soft. I couldn't help the pity I felt for the actor.

Eli glanced over at me. "Please don't feel sorry for me. I don't deserve it. Blake is gone, and there's nothing I can do to bring him back. That's on me—I don't want anyone else suffering for it."

I shook my head. "No, not that. I mean, that's sad too, but I meant that all this time you thought Christopher was doing you a favor. You've probably been leaning on him during this difficult time, and he's been the friend you needed. Except it wasn't him who was doing you a favor—*you* were the one covering for *him*."

22

E li gave me a blank look. "I'm sorry?"

Dottie and Sheriff Hart were giving me similar looks, but Christopher? He looked scared.

"Christopher wasn't your alibi," I said. "You were Christopher's. You both gave the same story, but do you know what Christopher was actually doing right before the explosion?"

Eli glanced at his friend. "No, I don't."

Christopher met my gaze. "Do *you*?"

I shook my head. "No. I don't have the faintest idea. But I do know some things. I know that Eli just told us you were seen walking toward your trailer before the explosion. I know that you weren't responding to anyone on their radios after the explosion, because Jennifer tried reaching out to you. I know that Frederick had been in the vicinity of your trailer at some point, because he dropped his lighter there. I also know that Frederick was causing a lot of problems on your set and Leanne had told him to go home. I believe that you told him the same thing.

Screenwriters aren't meant to be on set—it only causes problems. Leanne was on standby at the bed and breakfast if you needed any last-minute revisions—you valued her input. But Frederick—he was delaying production, which mean he was costing you money."

Christopher remained silent. I took that to mean I was on the right track.

"And because I doubt that Frederick works for free, he probably also wanted you to pay him for his expertise," I continued. "All the more reason to send him packing." I paused. "What I can't figure out is why you would shoot Blake Sommer. You hadn't even been introduced to him yet. Unless you had already been made privy to the existence of Eli's brother and you wanted to take care of him before he also became a problem."

Sheriff Hart raised an eyebrow and leaned over to whisper in my ear, "Blake wasn't shot."

I stepped back so I could read his expression. His gaze remained steady—he was serious. "What about the bullet casing in your evidence drawer?"

The sheriff shook his head. "That bullet wasn't used to kill Blake. It was used to puncture the propane tank. We also found evidence of gasoline poured around the tank to help the flames along. The killer probably hoped the tank would burst open with the explosion, hiding evidence of the bullet hole, but things rarely work like they do in the movies."

That meant that Blake hadn't been targeted at all.

That changed everything.

I turned to face Christopher.

"You thought that Blake was Frederick, didn't you? You probably asked Frederick to meet you there, but you had to remain at a distance when you caused the explosion. It wasn't until after Blake was identified and you saw that Frederick was alive and well that you realized your mistake. That's when you decided you had to finish the job where you knew you couldn't miss." I paused. "What was your motive for killing him? He was costing you time and money, but I don't know if that was enough to kill him over —everyone knew that Frederick was difficult to work with. What did he do, threaten you?"

Christopher tilted his head to the side. "Who are you again?"

Deflection. I could work with that.

"I'm Jo Darby," I said, sticking out a hand. "My sister and I own Sandcastle Bakery." I waited for him to shake my hand.

He didn't.

"They have very good beignets," Eli said. "I passed them around to the crew, but I don't think you were there."

Christopher didn't even bother acknowledging Eli. His gaze flickered over to Dottie, who was behind us all and seemed to be trying to stay out of the conversation.

"Why are you here?" Christopher asked, his attention returning to me.

"That's a very good question," Sheriff Hart asked.

I ignored him. "Because my sister and I are going to help put you in jail, where you belong."

Christopher smiled. "I know you don't have proof. Otherwise, your sheriff would have arrested me already."

Darn. That was true.

I turned to Jennifer. So far, she was the only one who hadn't lied to me. "Does anyone on the production crew have a gun? Maybe someone who has it for self-defense or something."

She wrinkled her nose. "Why would anyone bring a gun here to the smallest town in California? It's hardly dangerous. Not to mention that we're working twelve hours a day, sometimes more. We barely have time to eat and sleep."

Jennifer hadn't answered my question, so I stayed silent and waited for it.

She released a sigh and waved a hand through the air. "I can't be one hundred percent certain, but no, as far as I know, no one brought a gun. I've never seen one or heard talk of one. Like I said, what would be the point? If we were shooting the film in downtown LA, we might be having a different conversation, but look where we are."

"And there wasn't a gun on set," I mumbled. "That we know of. It's a chaotic environment, so who knows anything anymore?"

Dottie sensed where I was going with this, and her gaze snapped to the sheriff. "How often do you check your security cameras?"

Sheriff Hart wouldn't have answered that question if I had asked it, but I knew he would for Dottie.

"Only when I have reason to. Why?"

She nodded, as though she had expected as much. "Did anyone stop by your office the day of the explosion? Or maybe the day before."

Sheriff Hart ran a hand through his hair. "Honestly, I have no idea. Ever since filming began, Deputy Randy and I are out wandering the town most of the day. Half the town has been thrilled that Hollywood is filming a movie here, and the other half have logged noise complaints and reported suspicious characters. People want to know we are keeping an eye on things, and it's our job to convince them that the film crew has no interest in stealing their property."

Dottie didn't look surprised. "And do you lock the doors to the sheriff's office before going out on the town?"

From the many times I'd stopped by the sheriff's office, I knew he didn't.

"Sometimes," he admitted. "When I remember. But honestly, there's nothing of interest in there."

I raised a hand. "What about your evidence drawer in your desk?"

He tossed a glance my way, his lips pulling into a

frown. "Why does it feel like I'm the one under investigation here?"

Yup, I should have left it to Dottie.

But my sister had my back.

"Because, as far as I know, you are the only one with a gun in this town," Dottie said. "And if these two deaths weren't premeditated before the killer arrived in Starlight Ridge, and it appears they weren't, the killer would need to get a gun from somewhere."

Sheriff Hart was now looking agitated with my sister—a rarity for him. "If you're insinuating that they took my gun, I assure you I keep it on me at all times. It's part of my uniform and I'm never without it, no matter how unlikely it is that I would ever need to use it." He held Dottie's gaze. "You have a gun, don't you?"

Dottie smiled. "I do. And it is kept under lock and key in a gun case in my bedroom. Who else in town owns a gun?"

"No one." And then the sheriff's eyes widened. "I'll be right back." He walked toward the back of the chocolate shop while keeping us in his eyeline.

"What is he doing?" I asked Dottie, careful to keep my voice low.

"He's calling Deputy Randy," she said, the corners of her lips pulling up.

"Why?"

Never mind. I knew exactly why.

I turned to Christopher. "Really? You would take advantage of a sweet guy like that? What did you do, ask him what the fire escape routes were for the town, then take his gun while he was looking in the back to see if they had a binder for that?"

Everyone just stared at me, including Dottie. I cleared my throat. "Hypothetically speaking, of course. Everyone knows a town doesn't have fire escape routes. You just... leave."

Christopher shook his head. "Of course not—"

Sheriff Hart returned, his brows furrowed. "It's confirmed. Deputy Randy's gun is missing. Strangely enough, he said that you, Christopher, visited a couple days ago. Apparently, you wanted to check in and make sure the residents of our town didn't have any issues with the film crew. You'd heard rumors that our town wasn't happy with how they were handling things, what with our not being able to hang Christmas decorations and all that."

"Yes, because I'm considerate," Christopher said. "That certainly can't be grounds for thinking I'm a murderer."

Sheriff Hart smiled. "It's not."

Christopher released a long breath. "Well, thank goodness we got that cleared up."

"He also remembers," the sheriff continued, "that you asked about why he didn't wear a gun. He told you that he doesn't like guns but was required to purchase one as part of the job—we don't have the budget to issue official ones

—so he keeps it locked up in his desk. But of course, you noticed the deputy never locks his desk."

I thought back to when I'd needed to close the deputy's drawer just that evening when I'd borrowed his phone. The man had been using his desk and never even noticed that his gun was missing. The poor guy was going to get an earful when the sheriff returned.

"I asked the deputy to review the security tapes from the day in question," Sheriff Hart said. "You asked if there was a restroom you could use, and when Deputy Randy got up to show you where it was, you opened the drawer, pulled his gun out, and stuck it in the waist of your pants."

A tense silence fell over the room.

"Security cameras?" Christopher asked, his voice weak. "I didn't think that was a thing here in Starlight Ridge."

"It isn't," the sheriff said. "Except in my office. Just got them installed a couple months ago." He glanced at me. "Isn't that right, Jo?"

I gave him an embarrassed smile. "It is, and we're so grateful to know that our sheriff here is keeping us safe." I turned a glare on Christopher. "How dare you use Randy's good nature against him. He's as wonderful a person as they come—you would have made him the primary suspect in this case if you hadn't wiped off all the prints. Bad luck for Leanne picking it up after you'd left it by the body. You still hoped it would point to Deputy Randy as the guilty party, though, didn't you?"

Dottie looked to the sheriff. "I don't want to be critical, but why didn't you run the serial number through the gun registry? You would have saved yourself a lot of headaches."

"Because California doesn't have a firearm registration requirement, and Christopher was counting on Deputy Randy to have failed to register his gun." He added quietly, "Even though I asked him to."

Sheriff Hart then grabbed Chritopher's wrist and slapped handcuffs on him. "You have the right to remain silent."

"Wait," I said, stepping forward. "We still don't know why Christopher killed Frederick."

Christopher remained silent. Smart move on his part.

"Because in this business, there is no loyalty," Dottie answered in his stead. "It doesn't matter what you've done in the past. It doesn't matter how great you were. No matter how talented a screenwriter Frederick had been, he was now unpredictable. He kept showing up, uninvited, and costing the production money. Everyone saw that Christopher had no control over the screenwriter. Reputation is everything in this industry, and if things continued in this manner, no one in the industry would want to work with Christopher. He couldn't get Frederick to leave, so he had to come up with another way."

Eli Hunt stood off to the side, shaking his head and looking heartbroken. "I thought of you as a brother," he murmured. He glanced up at the director. "I would have defended you to the ends of the earth."

Christopher gave him a sad smile. "I know. Why do you think you were my alibi?"

And then Sheriff Hart led him away.

3 WEEKS LATER

It was a gorgeous day, and I didn't think anything could make it better except Leanne's enchiladas. Dottie and I, however, hadn't even made it up the steps to the bed and breakfast when the front door swung open and Leanne came bounding out. Skittles leaped back and tried to find cover, instead wrapping me with her leash.

"Isaac and I are getting married," Leanne squealed, enfolding us both in a tight hug.

I laughed and hugged her back, even as I tried not to lose my balance. "That's wonderful. When is the big day?"

Leanne pulled back. "In two weeks."

Dottie gaped. "That's so fast."

"We really didn't have a choice," Leanne said. "Ever since Eli took over directing, you never know what he's going to come up with. But he's added a wedding scene to *Amaretto*. Imagine this, it's the black moment of the film where everything is falling apart and Eli's character is so heartbroken that he crashes a wedding that his love interest is attending." She paused for dramatic effect and then let out another squeal. "Isaac and I are going to play the part of the bride and groom. I'm not sure if Isaac will be out of his wheelchair by then, but it doesn't matter to us, and Eli says it will only make the scene all the more powerful. It's all going to be so perfect."

Oh. So, they weren't getting married for real. They were acting like they were. That was nice, I supposed, but I was unsure why Leanne was so excited about it. Maybe, like me, she'd always dreamed of gracing the big screen. There was rarely any glory as a screenwriter—it was Eli Hunt who would have that honor.

When Leanne didn't get the reaction she was expecting, her smile dipped, and her gaze bounced between Dottie and me. "Why aren't you excited? You'll be invited, of course. The whole town will."

Dottie smiled and rested a hand on Leanne's arm. "That's wonderful, darling. We just thought you were getting married for real. But this sounds fun too."

Leanne's smile returned. "Oh, but we are. It will be a real pastor marrying us, so our wedding in the movie is going to be real. It will be immortalized forever."

Dottie and I both lit up, and even Skittles seemed to have forgiven Leanne, wandering back and rubbing Leanne's ankle with her head.

"That is fantastic news," I said. "Congratulations. After everything you've been through, you deserve it."

"I'm just grateful that *Amaretto* lived to see another day," Leanne said. "When the media descended on the town, I thought I was done for. There was no way the movie could survive two murders, and by the director of the film, no less. But Eli is not one to be deterred, and he used the coverage to our benefit. Now, they're expecting *Amaretto* to be the film of the year. That never happens with romances. We're always competing with the franchise movies—how could my story compete with the next superhero or Disney movie? And yet, here we are." She spun in a circle, indicating the area around us.

Leanne paused, her smile fading. "Oh, no. I just realized that you two are going on your big trip."

"We'll postpone," Dottie said with a smile. She didn't even need to check with me first, because she knew I'd agree. There was no way we were going to miss Leanne and Isaac's wedding for a little thing like a vacation.

"I can't ask you to do that," Leanne said. "After all you've done for me and Isaac, you deserve a relaxing getaway. Besides, you've already given us the best wedding gift we'll receive—our freedom."

"Please remember you said that when the only thing we get you is a nice card," I said. "But you can count on us being at your wedding. Thailand won't be very relaxing if we know what we're missing out on here."

"Not only that, but Jo has only managed to weasel her

way into an additional four scenes," Dottie said. "She won't be very happy if she misses out on her chance of being in a fifth. She's going to be the *Where's Waldo* of *Amaretto*."

I gave a solemn nod. "She's right."

Leanne laughed. "Well, we'd be honored if you can attend. Thank you." She paused. "I have to ask, though, why Thailand?"

I shrugged. "The nice young man who owns the hardware store said he's the only one in his family who is still here in Starlight Ridge. Everyone else is out building huts in Thailand. And I thought to myself, what an adventure. Dottie and I should go sometime. We've never even been outside the United States before, and that sounds like a fun place to start."

Leanne tilted her head to the side, looking confused. "You two are going to go build huts in Thailand?"

Even though I felt slightly offended that she didn't think we were up to it, it was understandable. We'd had to close the bakery for a week just to recover from the whole director-murdering-two-people ordeal.

Apparently, Dottie and Leanne were on the same page, because Dottie laughed at the thought of us building those huts. "No. Absolutely not. I don't do manual labor." She chuckled a bit more, before realizing that Leanne was waiting expectantly for her to continue. "We're actually going out there to meet a man."

Leanne stared. "A man," she repeated.

I nodded. "It was very serendipitous. Only a few days

after we'd talked to the young man at the hardware store, we met Matteo. Now we have both a place to stay and a tour guide."

"Did you meet this man online?" Leanne asked, her words slow. I didn't understand why she looked so concerned.

"We did," Dottie said brightly. "It's actually a funny story. Autumn had offered to help Jo and I get onto one of those social media places; she thought it would be good for networking, though I didn't understand what the point of all that was. We've been doing just fine on our own. Wouldn't you know it, there is an entire group dedicated to business owners who have opened a French bakery. It's not a big group, just five or six people, including Dottie and I, but most of them have opened their bakeries in small towns, just like us. There is a man on there, Matteo, who opened a French bakery in a town in Thailand. Apparently, he does quite well. So, we're going to go out and learn from him."

"So...you're going out to meet a stranger in a country where you don't speak the language." If anything, Leanne seemed more worried than before.

"No, not a stranger," I said, trying to hide my impatience. "Matteo. The others in the group can't close their bakeries as easily as we can, or they would have met us there as well. But it's going to be wonderful. Matheo has already promised to take us to an elephant sanctuary. We won't ride them—apparently their training can be very cruel, and we don't want to be a part of something like that."

"And Autumn is okay with this?" Leanne asked.

"She's getting the week off and she gets to spend it all with Skittles, why wouldn't she be?" I then noticed that Dottie's expression had opened, and she seemed to understand something that I didn't.

"You're worried that he's not who he says he is." Dottie smiled. "That's sweet of you. But you didn't think I would go half-way across the world unless I'd done a full background check on him, did you?"

Leanne's lips parted, and then she chuckled, seeming thoroughly amused by this. "I should have remembered that you two are perfectly capable of taking care of yourselves." She folded her arms across her chest. "So, it's a work trip. Not you two relaxing on a beach with a couple of Thai mojitos."

"Oh, there will be plenty of relaxing," I assured her.

"That's right, you're going to the elephant sanctuary," Leanne said. "That sounds amazing. You're sure that Matteo is okay with you two coming a little later than you had planned?"

"Yes. He said he'd love to have us anytime."

"Wonderful. Isaac will be so happy to hear that you'll be able to attend the wedding. Now," she turned back toward the bed and breakfast, "what do you say we get you those enchiladas that I know you came for?"

"Couldn't think of anything better," Dottie said. She

then walked right up the steps—without using the banister. She didn't seem to have noticed what a big deal that was for her, but rather than freak her out by pointing it out, I stayed silent.

Instead, I smiled.

Today was a perfect day. A walk with my sister and Skittles. News of a wedding. Enchiladas. And Dottie was getting stronger, just in time for our life-changing adventure.

If only things could stay this way forever.

Or at least until we got back from Thailand.

Even as I thought it, I knew Dottie and I were never that lucky.

The End

CHOOSE YOUR OWN ADVENTURE:
MYSTERY OR ROMANCE

MADDIE SWALLOWS MYSTERIES:

New Mexican Cozy Mystery

Dead Before Dinner

Dead Upon Arrival

Dead Before I Do

Dead Among Stars

Dead by Design

Dead in the Dark

Dead Without a Hitch

Dead by the Outlaw's Noose

SEASIDE FRENCH PATISSERIE MYSTERIES

Death and Dacquoise

Poison and Pudding

Bullets and Beignets

Murder and Madeleines

BORROWING AMOR: New Mexican Romance

Borrowing Amor

Borrowing Love

Borrowing a Fiancé

Borrowing a Billionaire

Borrowing Kisses

Borrowing Second Chances

STARLIGHT RIDGE: Beach Romance

Diving into Love

Resisting Love

Starlight Love

Building on Love

Winning his Love

Returning to Love

Fearless Love

ABOUT THE AUTHOR

Kat Bellemore is the author of both the Borrowing Amor small town romance series and the Maddie Swallows cozy mystery series. Deciding to have New Mexico as the setting for these series was an easy choice, considering its amazing sunsets, blue skies and tasty green chile. That, and she currently lives there with her husband and two cute kids. They hope to one day add a dog to the family, but for now, the native animals of the desert will have to do. Though, Kat wouldn't mind ridding the world of scorpions and centipedes. They're just mean.